DAWN'S BIG DATE

Speaking of good ideas—I had one just as I was falling asleep that night. In my mind, I was going over all the things that had been said that evening. I remembered saying that maybe everyone should leave Norman alone.

Then I thought of Lewis.

If Mary Anne had left me alone, I could have conducted my date with him my way. I was pretty sure it would have worked out a lot better.

Isn't it funny how you can see things about someone else that you can't see about yourself? I knew Norman needed everyone to stop interfering. But I hadn't realized it was exactly what *I* needed, too.

I made up my mind. I had to find some way to see Lewis again. Alone.

Dawn's *so* nervous about Lewis Bruno's visit to Stoneybrook. What if he doesn't like her? What if she's too plain? Dawn decides she needs a new image—lots of make-up, tight clothes. She could even learn how to *flirt*. But will Lewis and the rest of the Babysitters like the new Dawn?

Scholastic Children's Books,
Scholastic Publications Ltd,
7–9 Pratt Street, London NW1 0AE, UK

Scholastic Inc.,
555 Broadway, New York, NY 10012-3999, USA

Scholastic Canada Ltd,
123 Newkirk Road, Richmond Hill,
Ontario, Canada L4C 3G5

Ashton Scholastic Pty Ltd,
P O Box 579, Gosford, New South Wales,
Australia

Ashton Scholastic Ltd,
Private Bag 92801, Penrose, Auckland,
New Zealand

First published in the US by Scholastic Inc., 1992
First published in the UK by Scholastic Children's Books, 1994

ISBN 0 590 55488 3

Typeset in Plantin by Contour Typesetters, Southall, London
Printed by Cox & Wyman Ltd, Reading, Berks.

10 9 8 7 6 5 4 3 2

DAWN'S BIG DATE

Ann M. Martin

*The author gratefully acknowledges
Suzanne Weyn
for her help in
preparing this manuscript.*

1st CHAPTER

"Oh, no!" cried Mary Anne Spier. "Please tell me you're not going to make that." She was staring down at the health food cookbook I held in my lap. Her eyes were wide with horror. "Dawn, I really don't think anyone will want to eat tofu apple nut loaf at this party," she added.

"Okay," I said, flipping through the pages. "We could try this one. Soyabean pie."

Mary Anne sighed deeply. "Soyabeans in a pie? I bet there's not even a teaspoon of sugar in it, either."

"Nope. Honey."

"You and I have totally different taste buds," said Mary Anne, as she plopped down into the chair next to mine. "Let me look at this book. Maybe I can find something in here that isn't completely gross."

It was the day before New Year's Eve,

and we were in our kitchen, deciding what to serve at our New Year's Eve sleepover party. I'm using the word *our* because Mary Anne and I live together (along with our parents, of course). We're stepsisters. But before we became stepsisters, we were best friends.

Maybe I'd better start at the beginning. First let me introduce myself. My name is Dawn Schafer. I'm originally from California. A while ago I moved here to Stoneybrook, Connecticut, with my mother and my younger brother, Jeff.

Mum came back to Stoneybrook after she and my dad got divorced. Stoneybrook is where she grew up. Pop-pop and Granny (Mum's parents) still live here. I suppose that made Mum feel a little more secure, since the divorce was hard on her at first.

Unfortunately, Mum was the only one who was happy about the move. Jeff and I really missed California. I missed my friends and the warm weather, and everything Californian.

There was only one thing I liked about Stoneybrook right from the start. Our house. It was built in 1795. Can you imagine? The doorways are low, the staircases are narrow, and the rooms are small and dark. It is the total opposite of the sunny ranch-style house we left back in California. But for some reason I loved our new (old) house straight away.

2

And here's the best part. Our house has a secret passage that leads from the barn in the back garden right into my bedroom! It was probably once part of the Underground Railroad, which helped slaves from the South escape to freedom in the North. How's that for total coolness!

Anyway, even though the house was great, I wasn't too sure about the rest of Stoneybrook. Then I met Mary Anne. It didn't take long for us to become best friends.

At first glance, Mary Anne certainly didn't look like somebody who would become my best friend. Her brown hair was in plaits, and she always wore these awful little-kid pinafore dresses. Since she's on the short side, she appeared much younger than a seventh-grader. Which is what she was. (So was I. Now we're both in the eighth grade.)

Mary Anne and I must have made a pretty odd couple. There she was, short and sort of babyish. And there I was, tall, with long (waist-length) white-blonde hair, and my own style of dressing. (My friends call it California casual.)

Still, despite looks, there's a lot to like about Mary Anne. She's extremely sensitive and a great listener. Talking to her felt very natural and easy. And as we got to know each other better, two things happened that I would never have expected.

3

The first thing was that Mary Anne introduced me to the members of the BSC (Babysitters Club). They were Mary Anne's friends (she had fallen out with them when we first met, but that didn't last long) and now they're my friends, too. They asked me to join the BSC almost straight away, and I've been a member ever since. The BSC has become one of the most important things in my life. It's the reason I eventually came to like Stoneybrook. I'll tell you more about it later.

The second unexpected thing was that Mary Anne and I discovered our parents had gone out together when they were at high school. More than that—they were in *love*! We could tell by the romantic stuff they wrote to each other in their yearbooks. (We found my mother's yearbook first. It was still packed in a box, even though we'd been in Stoneybrook a while. My mother is not exactly the most efficient, organized person in the world, to put it mildly.)

Things didn't work out between my mum and Mary Anne's dad back then. That was mostly because my grandparents didn't think Richard (Mary Anne's father) would ever be successful, since he was from a poor family. (Their words.) They did everything to break them up, including sending Mum to college in California. Their plan worked—almost. Mum met my dad in California. And Richard also married

4

someone else, who became Mary Anne's mum.

But then, as you know, Mum became single again. And Mary Anne's mother died when Mary Anne was little, so Richard was also single. With a small push from Mary Anne and me, they started seeing each other again. (They went out together for ages and ages.) Finally, though, they got married. Now we all live in the old farmhouse together. That's how Mary Anne and I became best friends *and* stepsisters.

It sounds perfect, doesn't it? Mostly it is. It would be totally perfect if my brother, Jeff, were still here. But he never adjusted to Stoneybrook the way I did. One day he asked to go back and live with my father in California. It was very hard on all of us to let him go, but we knew it was for the best. And even though I sometimes go to California to visit, I still miss Jeff.

On that particular day, though, Jeff was here visiting for a winter holiday. He'd been a total pest since the second he got off the plane. The only reason we had quiet at that moment was because he'd gone off to visit his friends the Pike triplets. (Truthfully, I didn't mind his pestiness. It felt as if he'd never left.)

Besides Jeff's going to California, we had a few other problems with the divorce and the remarriage. Mum had to get used to Tigger, Mary Anne's kitten. Mary Anne and I had to get used to sharing a room (which didn't work out, and now we have our own rooms). And then there was the big food issue. That's what we were faced with as we tried to plan our party.

Mum and I eat healthy things like raw vegetables, tofu, and brown rice. The thought of eating red meat makes me want to throw up.

Mary Anne and Richard are completely opposite. It seems that they'll eat any old food. (Like hot dogs! Ugh, ugh. Yuck!) When it comes to eating, Mary Anne and Richard don't worry about their health much at all.

"These peanut butter log things might be okay," said Mary Anne doubtfully, as she pointed to a recipe in the book. "Only I wish we could use some ordinary peanut butter instead of that natural stuff."

"Look," I said, starting to get just a bit annoyed. "Why don't you make some snacks your way, and I'll make some my way. Then we'll see whose food gets eaten first."

"Good idea," said Mary Anne with a smile. "I want to have a go at those little hot dogs wrapped in biscuit dough. And I saw this recipe for individual pepperoni pizzas that you make on English muffins."

"Yuck," I groaned, as I covered my mouth and puffed up my cheeks.

Mary Anne shook her head. "How can

you say that? I love those little hot dogs. They're so adorable. What's that cute name they call them? Oh, yeah, pigs-in-a-blanket." She glanced at the clock on the wall. It was almost three. "We'd better start writing our shopping lists," she reminded me. "Your mum told us to be ready at three-thirty to go food shopping."

Mum had gone to pick up Jeff at the Pikes'. (It was a Friday, but Mum's company had given her the day off for a long weekend.) "She'll probably be late," I said. "You know how much she likes gossiping with Mrs Pike."

Mary Anne looked worried. "I hope she's not too late. We have to get to our meeting later."

"Ohmigosh!" I cried. The holiday had put me so off schedule that I had almost forgotten it was a Friday. We always have BSC meetings on Mondays, Wednesdays, and Fridays, from 5:30 until 6:00.

Mary Anne took two sheets of paper and two pencils from the kitchen junk drawer and handed one of each to me. We both began writing lists of supplies we'd need for the party.

"I talked to Logan today," said Mary Anne, as she wrote.

"That's nice," I commented, not even looking up from my writing. This wasn't exactly earthshaking news. Mary Anne talks to Logan every day. Logan is her steady boyfriend. (From the way I've described Mary Anne, it might seem strange that she has a boyfriend. I should explain that although Mary Anne is still shy, she no longer wears pinafore dresses and pigtails. Richard has eased up on the fashion rules. Mary Anne has grown a few inches, too. She doesn't look like a little kid any more.) Anyhow, Logan and Mary Anne are very close.

"Lewis called him last night. He's definitely coming in mid-January, but he's not sure of the exact date yet," she continued. "It's too bad he couldn't come while we're off school. But his school is on a different schedule, so he didn't have any choice. I'm sure we'll have fun, though . . ."

Mary Anne was talking, but I was no longer listening. I was too busy worrying about Lewis.

Lewis Bruno is Logan's cousin. He lives in Louisville, Kentucky. That's where Logan is from originally. A while ago, Lewis and I started writing to each other. Mary Anne and Logan set it up. They were sure Lewis and I would get along great. They sent him my picture (without asking me). Then Lewis sent me a picture of himself. He's really cute. And, from his letters, I could tell he was really nice. Every time one of his letters appeared in the postbox I'd feel excited and happy. He always had something funny or interesting to say.

So, what was the problem? *I* was the problem. Even though Lewis had seen my photo, and even though he seemed to enjoy my letters, I was afraid he wouldn't like me. I know this sounds as if I'm totally insecure, but I'm not. People are always saying what an *individual* I am. You have to be at least somewhat secure to be an individual.

It was just that no boy had ever liked me. Not the way Logan liked Mary Anne. (There was one time I thought a boy called Travis was interested in me. But he wasn't. He was just leading me on, probably because he could tell I had a major crush on him.)

Other girls are always saying I should be a model or an actress. They say, "Oh, I wish I had your silky hair." Or, "I'd die to have your skin." (*They* might have good hair and skin if they didn't eat so much junk food.) Enough people have told me I'm pretty, so I should believe it. Personally, though, I can't see it. To me, I just look like me. Not pretty, not ugly—just me.

Obviously, boys couldn't see it, either. They liked me well enough to borrow my notebook or to mess around with. But when it came to really liking me, forget it.

"Dawn! You're not writing!" said Mary Anne, interrupting my thoughts. "You

9

weren't listening to me, either. What are you thinking about?"

"Lewis," I admitted. "Mary Anne, what if he hates me?"

"Hates you!" gasped Mary Anne. "That's insane. I don't know anybody who hates you."

"You know what I mean, though. What if he's really disappointed when he meets me? He seems so nice. I want him to think I'm, you know, attractive."

"Don't worry," Mary Anne said, putting her hand on my arm. "He's already seen your photo."

"I suppose so," I admitted.

"Look, you two must have exchanged at least a zillion letters so far," continued Mary Anne. "He knows plenty about you. It hasn't stopped him from writing."

Mary Anne is great to talk to, as I said before. For the moment, I felt less worried. "I'm going to go upstairs and make it a zillion and one letters," I said.

"What about your list?" asked Mary Anne.

"I know what I need," I assured her.

"I do, too," Mary Anne said, wrinkling her nose. "Honey, nuts, soyabeans, and two tonnes of tofu."

"Three tonnes," I teased, as I headed out of the kitchen.

Upstairs I opened a new packet of writing paper. Each sheet had a tiny silver unicorn in the right hand corner. Jeff had bought it for me in California. Here's what I wrote:

Dear Lewis,
   Hi! Mary Anne just told me you'll be here in January. All right! Get ready for the adventure of a lifetime. Stoneybrook, land of a thousand thrills. I wish. But, seriously, I am really looking forward to meeting you. Mary Anne and Logan have been planning what the four of us will do when you get here. I get pooped just listening to them. Yesterday Logan brought over a film timetable from the newspaper. He'd circled the film he wants us to see.

I stopped writing because I'd heard the front door open and close. In a moment my mother called up the stairs. "Dawn, come on!"

"Okay, be right there," I called back.

I started writing very fast.

Got to run. Mum's calling. Mary Anne and I have to go shopping for our New Year's Eve sleepover party. All the members of the BSC are coming. My brother Jeff has invited the Pike triplets. It should be crazy but fun. I hope you have a very happy New Year. I can't wait to see you.

'Bye for now,
Dawn

I stuck the letter in an envelope and ran down the stairs. Mum, Mary Anne, and Jeff were in the kitchen. It was weird to see Jeff with his sun-bleached hair and light tan, all bundled up in a jacket. He was putting a cup of soup into the microwave.

Mum was rummaging through the junk drawer. "The supermarket is having a sale on sparkling cider," she said. "I cut the coupons out. I know they're in here somewhere."

I went to the hall cupboard and got my jacket.

"Are these the ones you mean?" I heard Jeff ask, as I returned to the kitchen. He had found a plate in the microwave. The coupons were stuck to the bottom of the plate.

"Oh. Yes, they are," said my mother sheepishly. She looked at the three of us. Our expressions were somewhere between total exasperation and laughter. My mother

12

is *such* a scatterbrain.

"Okay, okay," she said, even though no one had said anything. She took the coupons from Jeff. "If it makes you all feel any better, my New Year's resolution is to become more organized."

"A resolution?" asked Jeff.

"Yeah. You know—when you decide to do something differently from the way you used to do it," Mary Anne explained. "People make resolutions on New Year's Eve because it's the beginning of a new year. It's like a new beginning."

A New Year's resolution. That made me think. What kind of resolution did *I* need to make?

2nd
CHAPTER

Kristy Thomas checked the time as Mary Anne and I scooted into Claudia Kishi's bedroom. "You're late," Kristy commented, pointing to Claudia's digital clock. The clock read 5:31. Kristy is a stickler for punctuality. She hates it if anyone is even one minute late for a Babysitters Club meeting.

"Sorry, we were shopping for the sleepover tomorrow," explained Mary Anne, who was now perched on the end of Claudia's bed.

"The checkout queues at the supermarket were humongous," I added, as I settled down, cross-legged on the floor.

There was this little bubble of tension in the room. I could tell from Kristy's expression that she was still annoyed. (I knew our being late wasn't the only thing that was bothering Kristy. She gets a little jealous of

14

me sometimes. Before I came along, she had been Mary Anne's only best friend.)

Luckily, Claudia broke the tension. "Now that we're all here I think we should have a pre-New Year's Eve celebration," she said, sliding gracefully off her bed.

She rolled a tin can the size of a small wastebasket out from under the bed. "Aunt Peaches ordered this for me. It came in the post yesterday," she said, popping open the lid. Inside were three different kinds of popcorn: ordinary, cheese, and caramel-coated, divided into compartments. Naturally, Claudia went straight for the caramel-coated. She is a total junk food fanatic.

"Wow! Cool! Popcorn!" cried Mal (Mallory) Pike, one of the two junior members of the BSC. Eagerly, she leaned forward from her spot on the floor and dug out a handful of cheese popcorn.

Our other junior member, Jessi (Jessica) Ramsey, was sitting beside Mal. She practically dived into the caramel-coated popcorn. "This is a great present," said Jessi. "Your aunt really knows what you like."

Claudia nodded, her mouth full. "It was lucky I was at home to receive it," she said, clearing her throat. "I took it right upstairs before my parents saw the caramel-coated and cheese popcorn. I've only just talked them into letting me have ordinary popcorn. Flavoured popcorn would definitely

15

be out." (Claudia always hides her junk food because her parents don't approve of it.)

"Hey, if you lot could stop stuffing your faces for a minute, we have some business to discuss," Kristy reminded us sternly.

"We can eat and do business at the same time," said Stacey McGill, stretching from her spot on the bed to scoop up a small amount of plain popcorn. She ate it slowly, one piece at a time.

Maybe this would be a good time to tell you something about each member of the club.

You already know about Mary Anne, so I'll start with Kristy. She's the chairman because the club was her idea. Also because she's a natural chairman-type. (To put it more plainly—she's very bossy.) Even though Kristy comes on too strong sometimes, deep down she's sensitive and nice. Plus, she's pretty level-headed and knows how to get things done. Kristy is also great with little kids.

There's something about Kristy that you would never guess. She's rich! Her step-father, Watson Brewer, is a real millionaire. Her family lives in an actual mansion. It's unbelievably gorgeous.

Kristy certainly doesn't look like my idea of a rich kid. Jeans, a sweater over a poloneck, and trainers—that's Kristy's idea of fashion. She gives her long, brown hair a few quick strokes with a hairbrush and think she's gone all out. (Since she's short, she's often mistaken for being younger than she is.)

Kristy doesn't act like a rich kid, either. You couldn't find a more normal, down-to-earth person. She loves sports and even coaches a little kids' softball team called Kristy's Krushers.

I suppose Kristy isn't a typical rich kid because she wasn't always rich. Her mother didn't marry Watson until Kristy had finished the seventh grade. Before that, Kristy's family wasn't poor, but they weren't loaded, either. Kristy's father just walked out when Kristy was little, leaving her mother to support the whole family. (Kristy hardly ever hears from her father. She says she doesn't care, but it's got to hurt.) Her mum must have had it tough. Kristy has two older brothers and a younger brother. Four kids is a lot for one person to take care of all by herself.

Kristy's mother works hard, though. She has a good job with a company in Stamford. I think that's how she met Watson.

Since Watson came along, Kristy's mum's life is much easier, although she now has even *more* kids. Watson has two little kids, a boy and a girl from a previous marriage. They stay with the Brewers every other weekend, for some holidays, and for two weeks in the summer. *And* (as if the house wasn't full enough) they adopted a little girl from Vietnam. Emily Michelle is two and a half, and so cute you can hardly stand it. Then Nannie (Kristy's mother's mother) moved in to help out with the kids. With all those people living together, I suppose it's a good thing that they *do* live in a mansion.

The vice-chairman of our club is Claudia. She gets to be VC mostly because we hold meetings in her room. Claudia has the best room for meetings because she is the only member with her own phone *and* her own phone number. When I tell you about how the club works, you'll see that having a private phone line is very important. (More about the club later.)

The first thing most people notice about Claudia is her appearance. She's naturally beautiful with long, shiny, straight black hair. (She's Japanese-American, so her hair is really *black*-black, not just dark brown.) And she has delicate features. But what strikes people about Claudia even more than her stunning looks is her sense of fashion.

Claudia wears super-trendy clothes, and she puts them together in ways that are uniquely Claudia. Today, for example, she was wearing maroon leggings and ballet slippers under a baggy yellow shirt. Around her waist she wore this great belt that she made herself from three thin strips of leather tied together and decorated with ceramic beads. For the final touch, Claudia had swept her hair over to one side and tied it up with another thin leather strip that had the same kind of beads on it. She looked great—and she was just hanging around her own house!

Claudia's fashion sense is an extension of her artistic talent. Claudia loves to do anything artistic: sketch, paint, sculpt, make pottery and jewellery.

When Claudia grows up I'm sure she'll be either an artist or a fashion designer. Which is lucky for her. I don't think she'd do too well at a profession that required a lot of qualifications. Claudia is a terrible pupil. (Straight C's, if she's lucky. And she can't spell for toffee.) The odd thing about Claudia being a poor student is 1. she's really clever and 2. her older sister, Janine, is a real-life genius. Claudia's parents used to pressure her constantly to be more like Janine, but Claudia wasn't interested. (Even though they've let up a bit, I still think Claud's parents are too hard on her. She has to hide her Nancy Drew books because her parents think they're "frivolous." I mean, come on. At least she's *reading*.)

Claudia's best friend, and the treasurer of the BSC, is Stacey. Like Claudia, she's also fashion conscious. Her clothes are very cool, but she doesn't put them together quite as

19

originally as Claudia does. Still, she always looks great. She's tall and thin with big blue eyes. Her fluffy, shoulder-length blonde hair is permed and suits her perfectly. Of all of us, Stacey seems the most grown-up.

Maybe that's because Stacey has had a tough life. She has diabetes, which means her body has trouble controlling the level of sugar in her blood. She has to stay on a very strict diet. Also, she has to give herself injections of insulin every day. (Even thinking about that gives me the creeps!)

Stacey has been bounced around a lot, too. First she moved from New York City to Stoneybrook (her father was transferred here). Then her father was transferred *back* to New York. *Then* her parents decided to get divorced, and Stacey moved back to Stoneybrook with her mother. *Whew*! That's a lot of moving. But we are thrilled that she's back.

I was especially thrilled. Not only because I missed Stacey when she left, but also because I had taken over her job as treasurer. You see, I'm the alternate officer of the club, which means I can take over for any member whenever I'm needed. That's how I got the treasurer's job, even though I'm not *too* great in the maths department. Stacey is a whiz at it, though. I was glad to hand the job back to her.

We also have two junior members. They're called "junior" because they're only eleven. (The rest of us are thirteen.) They can't sit at night unless it's for their own sisters and brothers. But they do babysit in the afternoons. That frees the rest of us to sit in the evenings.

Besides age, Mal and Jessi have a lot in common. They're both nuts about horses and books. (As you might imagine, they're wild about horse books in particular.) They're both the oldest kids in their families. Oh, and they're best friends.

They're not clones, though. Each girl has a distinct personality. Another difference is that Mal is white and Jessi is black. When the Ramseys first moved to Stoneybrook, some people gave them a hard time simply because they're black. Thank goodness that died down. Now the Ramseys are settled in and seem happy.

Besides her parents, Jessi lives with her aunt; her sister, Becca (eight); and her baby brother, Squirt. (His real name is John Philip Ramsey, Jr., but he was so small at birth that the nurses in the hospital nick-named him Squirt.)

The most amazing thing about Jessi is her dancing ability. She plans to be a ballerina and has already performed in several professional productions. She's incredibly talented.

Mal is also talented in her own way. Her ambition is to write and illustrate children's books. I know she'll be great at it because she's very creative. And she certainly knows what kinds of stories interest kids. She's the oldest of eight! The combination of her creativity and her experience with all those brothers and sisters makes her a terrific babysitter.

And, just so you'll know, we also have two associate members: Kristy's friend Shannon Kilbourne and Logan Bruno. (That's right. Mary Anne's boyfriend.) Shannon and Logan don't come to meetings, but we call them as reserves if we have too many babysitting jobs.

Now that you know who's in the club, let me tell you how it works. As I said, we meet three times a week, for half an hour. Our clients know that we meet at those times. (At first the club advertised by distributing BSC leaflets. Now we're so popular we don't need to advertise any more. Though we do sometimes, anyway. Just to keep new clients coming.)

If a client needs a babysitter, he or she calls us during a meeting. (That's why Claudia's private phone is so important.) The great thing about this is that with one call, a client can reach seven experienced sitters. One of us is bound to be free to take the job.

That's where Mary Anne comes in. As club secretary she keeps track of the record book. In it she records everyone's schedule—Jessi's dance lessons, Mal's dental appointments, Claudia's art classes, and anything else that comes up. By checking her record book she can tell straight away who is free to accept a babysitting job.

That's not all she keeps in the record book. There's also a list of clients' names, addresses, and phone numbers. Plus a record of how much money we make, and each of our weekly sitting schedules. If we need to know anything, we can check with Mary Anne. She's a great secretary and has never, ever (not even once) made a mistake.

What do we do if the phone doesn't ring? Lots! For starters, on Mondays, Stacey collects the subs. That's the least fun part of the club. But it's necessary. We use the money to help pay Claudia's phone bill. And we pay Charlie, one of Kristy's older brothers, to drive her to meetings. (Kristy used to live across the street from Claudia. But Watson's mansion is on the other side of town.) We also buy new supplies for our Kid-Kits.

Kid-Kits were Kristy's idea and they're really helpful. A Kid-Kit is a box full of toys, colouring books, crayons, and other fun stuff. We often bring the Kid-Kits on babysitting jobs. The kids love them. There's something exciting about playing with new things. Even difficult kids settle down when we open our Kid-Kits.

If there's any money left over after all that, we splurge on a club pizza party or a sleepover or a trip to the cinema. Something fun.

After money business is settled, we sometimes go over our BSC notebook. This isn't the same as the record book. It's more like a diary for the club. We write down our babysitting experiences in the notebook. Sometimes it's a bit of a pain to do, but it is a helpful resource for all of us.

On that day we had plenty to do. We'd been so busy over the holidays that our Kid-Kits were in desperate need of restocking. Each of us was making suggestions for things to buy. Stacey was writing everything down and trying to work out what we could afford to buy and what we couldn't.

Mary Anne was the only one not making suggestions. She was busy writing in the BSC notebook. The night before, she'd sat for the Kormans. She was glad to report that Bill and Melody were no longer terrified of the toilet monster. (Believe it or not, the kids thought there was a monster in their toilet. Whenever it was flushed, they would race to their beds and hide.) Logan had suggested that Mary Anne make a game of it—like timing how fast Bill and Melody ran away, for example. Mary Anne tried it and it worked. Now the only problem was that the kids wouldn't *stop* flushing the toilet. They laughed hysterically every time they did. Oh, well.

As we were conducting the meeting, the phone rang. "Hello, Babysitters Club," Claudia answered. "Yes . . . yes . . . that's us." She took a pad and pencil off her desk and began writing down information. "Can I ask how you heard about us? . . . Oh, wow! Dr Johanssen is your paediatrician? Yeah, we babysit for her little girl, Charlotte, all the time. I'll find out who's available. . . . Great. I'll call you straight back."

"All right! A new client!" Kristy exclaimed after Claudia had hung up.

"Yeah," Claudia replied with a smile. "Dr Johanssen told this man Mr Hill that we're really good sitters."

Kristy shot Claudia a worried look. "He didn't ask for anyone in particular, did he?" she wanted to know. We're not supposed to work that way. Whoever's free gets the job.

"No, he didn't," Claudia said pointedly. "He just wants someone to look after his two kids, a nine-year-old girl and a seven-year-old boy."

Mary Anne already had the record book open. "When and what time?" she asked.

"Friday at four," Claudia read off her pad. "Mrs Hill won't be home from work, and Mr Hill has to go to a meeting. Normally he works at home."

"How about you, Dawn?" Mary Anne asked, looking up from the record book.

"Okay," I said. A nine-year-old and a seven-year-old. Usually those are pretty easy ages to sit for. That's what I thought, anyway, before I met Sarah and Norman Hill.

3rd
CHAPTER

"Hey, something smells good," said Richard, coming into the kitchen on Saturday afternoon. "What's cooking?"

"Don't get your hopes up, Dad," said Mary Anne, laughing. "It's a soyabean pie." She was standing at the worktop, rolling tiny hot dogs into "blankets" of dough. I was at the table, shaping peanut butter logs, while Jeff sprinkled them with coconut. Mum was at the worktop, arranging plastic utensils in paper cups.

"Oh . . . well, I'm sure it will be good," said Richard, his face falling. It fell even further as he gazed around the kitchen. It was a disaster area. Open packets, paper towels, dirty tea towels, used bowls and utensils were everywhere. Even Jeff was covered with tomato sauce. (He'd been helping Mary Anne with her English-muffin pizzas). Richard took a deep breath.

He's very different from my mother—super organized and neat.

I expected him to launch into his usual speech about "clearing up as you go" when cooking. He didn't, though. "I'm going up to the attic to look for those extra sleeping bags," he said, instead. I could tell from his distressed expression that he was trying hard not to plunge in and start whipping the kitchen into shape. I wondered if he'd made a New Year's resolution not to be such a neat freak.

"Thanks, darling," said my mother, as he left. In this spirit of compromise, Mum started wiping spilled sauce off the work surfaces and throwing old wrappers and boxes into a paper bag. (This was not her usual behaviour. Messes don't bother her in the least.) It was quite inspiring to see Richard and Mum trying so hard to make each other happy.

The rest of the day passed quickly. We cleared up the house, finished making the snacks and desserts, and decorated the living room. Mum pulled out a box filled with corny New Year's stuff—funny hats, horns, even a cardboard baby wearing a nappy, and a banner. The banner read, "1979." I hung it on the wall anyway, since I thought it was cool.

Soon it was seven o'clock. That's when we'd told everyone to come round. The first to arrive were Mal and the triplets, Adam,

Byron, and Jordan. The three of them are the same age as Jeff. The triplets are identical. Thank goodness they dress differently, though. Once you find out who is wearing what, you know who is who.

"Happy New Year—almost," said Mal, stepping into the living room with the triplets.

"Hey, you three," cried Jeff, hurrying to the door. The boys immediately ran off with Jeff, up to his room.

The next to arrive was Kristy. "Hi," she said, her sleeping bag on her shoulder and a shopping bag in her hand. "Where should I put this stuff?"

Mary Anne had come out of the kitchen. She took Kristy's jacket. "Your sleeping bag can go upstairs in Dawn's room. What's in the shopping bag?"

"Mum and Watson sent this stuff," said Kristy. She reached into the bag and pulled out a bottle and a small jar. "It's for your parents," she explained. "Champagne and caviar." There was also a bakery box at the bottom of the bag. "And these are some kind of special cookies for us."

"That was nice of them," I said, taking the bag.

"What is caviar, anyway?" Mal asked.

"Fish eggs," I told her.

Mary Anne and Kristy looked at each other. "Sounds yummy," Kristy said dryly, making a disgusted face.

"Have you ever tried it?" Mal asked me.

"No," I admitted. "It's supposed to be great, though."

"Adults eat the weirdest things," said Mary Anne.

In the next few minutes, Stacey and Claudia arrived. Naturally, they both looked gorgeous. Claudia had tied her hair up in a high ponytail with this silver netting around it. She was wearing wide black trousers and a top with a silver moon appliquéd on the front.

Stacey wore a close-fitting purple dress and pink tights with black stripes. "Wow! You two really got dressed up!" I said as they walked in. (I was dressed for comfort, in black leggings and a big blue top lined with fleece.)

"You have to get dressed up on New Year's Eve," said Claudia. "That's part of the fun."

I shrugged. I suppose everyone has their own idea of fun.

Jessi arrived next. Her father walked her to our front steps. My mother happened to come into the living room as I opened the door. "Happy New Year!" she said. "Richard and I are about to toast the New Year," she added to Jessi's dad. "Why don't you join us?"

"Sounds good," he replied, as Mum led him off to the kitchen, where she and Richard had been sitting.

"I'm so excited," said Jessi. "This will be the first time I've celebrated New Year's Eve. I've been sent to bed before midnight every other year."

As I took Jessi's coat, Stacey reached into her large black leather bag. "Mary Anne," she said in a sort of teasing singsong voice. "I have something to show you."

"What?" Mary Anne asked eagerly.

"I got a parcel in the post today from my father. He said it was a New York City care parcel." (Stacey is a real New York girl at heart, even though she likes Stoneybrook. On her bedroom wall she has a map of New York, a poster of the Empire State Building, and a poster of New York at night.) Stacey kept one hand in her bag as she spoke. "He sent me some really good sugarless chocolate from a gourmet shop near his flat. He also added these very cool sunglasses and hair clips that he bought from a street market. And he sent me this tape I asked him to look for." Stacey pulled the tape from her bag. "Ta-da! *Cam Geary Sings*!"

Mary Anne grabbed the tape from Stacey. "I don't believe it. I don't be-*leeeive* it!" she squealed. Cam Geary is Mary Anne's absolute favourite star. Even though he's an actor, I suppose he wanted to become a singer, too. *Cam Geary Sings* was his first recording. Mary Anne had read about it in a magazine and was dying to hear it. "I didn't think this was out yet. Where

31

did your father find it?" she asked.

"There's a huge record shop in town. They get everything first," Stacey told her.

We decided to go up to my room to listen to the tape. Mary Anne popped it into the stereo as everyone laid out their sleeping bags.

Nobody but Mary Anne thought much of Cam Geary's singing. "I think he sounds . . . good," she said loyally.

"This is only his first album. Maybe he's just sort of learning how to do it," Mal suggested.

For Mary Anne's sake we listened to the whole tape, but no one was paying attention after the first two songs. (Except Mary Anne, that is.) We started talking about school and babysitting. And about boys.

I've noticed lately that we talk about boys a lot more than ever before. Stacey and Claudia, especially. Even Kristy, who used to think boys are dweebs, is now interested.

"How are things with you and Logan these days?" Claudia asked Mary Anne.

"Great," Mary Anne replied with a bright smile. "We're having a lot of fun, now that he doesn't act as if he owns me." (Logan and Mary Anne broke up for a while because Logan was being possessive. But they missed each other too much to stay apart.)

"I wish I had a steady boyfriend," said Stacey with a sigh.

"I think Pete Black still likes you," said Kristy. Stacey went to a few dances with Pete, but they never really clicked.

"Pete is nicer than I thought," offered Mary Anne, looking up from the little booklet of lyrics that had come with the Cam Geary tape. "When I worked in that study group with him for English class, I saw his other side."

Stacey wrinkled her nose. "I don't know. He's too immature."

"You know who *is* adorable?" asked Claudia. "Arthur Feingold."

"Ugh!" cried Kristy. "He's too skinny."

"But don't you think Arthur has gorgeous hair?" Claudia replied.

"I don't think hair counts as much as eyes. Quint has wonderful eyes," Jessi said, sighing. Quint is a boy Jessi likes a lot. He likes her, too. I think you could say they're an *item*.

"I agree," said Mal. "Ben Hobart has great eyes. He also has an adorable nose. I *love* his nose." Mal has a super crush on Ben.

The one person not talking was me. I didn't have anything to add to the conversation. It's not that I wasn't interested in boys. I noticed the good looking, nice ones. But so far, no boy had really made me go crazy. (I take that back. Travis had, but he turned out to be a big dud, as I explained

33

earlier.) I was obviously doing something wrong.

As I listened, I was faintly aware of a strange sound. I stopped paying attention to the conversation and started concentrating on the sound. It was a scuffling noise. Were there squirrels or mice in the attic above us? No. The sound was coming from the bedroom wall. There was more scuffling and then—a giggle.

"What's the matter?" asked Kristy, noticing my expression.

Sliding off the bed, I put my finger to my lips. Everyone grew quiet as I crossed the room to the wall with the fancy moulding. I reached up and pressed the corner of the moulding. The wall swung open.

There, in the entrance to the secret passage, stood Jeff, Adam, Byron, and Jordan. They were wearing their jackets, since they'd had to go out to the barn to enter the passage. "Arthur Feingold is so cute!" Jeff teased.

"Just adorable!" added Jordan, running into the room.

"You little pests!" cried Mal. She jumped up and threw a pillow, hitting Adam.

The boys laughed. Jeff bounced on my bed. *"Claudia and Arthur sitting in a tree. K-I-S-S-I-N-G!"* he sang.

"Oh, I just *love* Ben Hobart's nose!" Adam taunted his sister.

"Out! Out!" I insisted, grabbing hold of Jeff. "You four little snoops, get out of here!"

At the same time, all the girls picked up pillows and drove the boys from the room. They ran, still laughing and teasing, into the landing and down the stairs.

"Anybody hungry?" asked Mary Anne. Of course, the answer was a rousing yes. We went down to the kitchen and began heating up the food we'd prepared. I had to admit that Mary Anne's little pizzas smelled good as they heated up.

Mr Ramsey had left by then. Mum and Richard helped us with the hot food. We'd already put out snacks of popcorn and pretzels, lemonade and sparkling cider. We'd been given permission to eat in front of the TV. We turned it on and watched what was happening in Times Square, in New York City. There were crowds of people blowing horns and cheering. Different rock bands played on an outdoor stage. "Boy, I miss the city at times like this," said Stacey, as she munched on a pretzel.

(By the way, Mary Anne and I tied in our food contest. Here's the score: Pizzas were a big hit; pigs-in-a-blanket were eaten by only half the group. Maybe because some of them burned slightly. My peanut butter logs were gobbled up instantly. But my soyabean pie was only half eaten. I thought it tasted like pumpkin pie. I suppose not everyone likes pumpkin pie, though.)

Finally it was midnight. Mum and Richard came downstairs. Jeff and the triplets ran up from the basement, where they'd been playing. Mum poured everyone some sparkling cider. We toasted and yelled "Happy New Year!" as the silver ball on the TV screen came down at midnight.

"Come on, you kids, bedtime," Mum said to Jeff and the triplets. Surprisingly, no one argued. The boys put down their horns and blowers right away. I noticed they looked very sleepy as they followed Mum and Richard upstairs.

"Now what should we do?" asked Kristy.

"I have an idea," said Claudia. "Let's each phone a boy and wish him Happy New Year! I'm phoning Arthur."

"You wouldn't!" cried Kristy, aghast.

"Why not," said Claudia boldly. "I think he likes me."

Stacey's big blue eyes narrowed thoughtfully. "Do you think I should phone Pete Black?"

"Yes," said Mary Anne. "You should give him another chance. But don't stay on long, because I want to call Logan."

Kristy looked at me and Mary Anne. "Would it be totally weird if I phoned Bart?" she asked.

"The Bart-Man? Of course not! I think he'd be flattered," said Mary Anne. Kristy and Bart Taylor like each other, but they were at that early, not-completely-definite-yet stage.

"Of course, call him. Why not?" said Claudia, swept up in the excitement.

"Why don't you phone Lewis?" Mary Anne suggested, turning to me.

I shook my head. "I'd feel too silly. I've never even met him. I'm going to start clearing up the kitchen."

Jessi and Mal volunteered to help. I think they felt funny about calling Quint or Ben. As the three of us worked, I tried to chat cheerfully. But that wasn't really how I felt. I was mortified! It was okay for Mal and Jessi to feel shy about calling a boy. They were only eleven.

From the living room, I could hear the phone conversations. Silence, then squeals of laughter between each call.

"Not fair! Not fair!" I heard Stacey protest. "You can't just yell 'Happy New Year, Bart-Man!' and hang up." Okay, so Kristy hadn't made the most romantic phone call. At least she could think of someone to call. I couldn't.

We spent the next hour talking and listening to music. It was almost one-thirty before we settled down. Everyone was just beginning to get drowsy when Kristy sat up in her sleeping bag. "Hey, we forgot to make New Year's resolutions," she said.

"What's yours?" Mary Anne asked her, leaning up on one elbow.

"Hmmmmmm." Kristy thought. "I resolve to make Kristy's Krushers the winning team this year. I was too easy on those kids last year. How about you, Mary Anne?"

"I'm going to try to be less shy. Sometimes it's hard on Logan when I'm too shy to go to parties or go out with kids I don't really know."

"Has he been complaining?" asked Kristy.

"No," said Mary Anne. "But remember when he went on those few dates with Cokie while we were split up? I think he enjoyed the fact that she was so outgoing. And I want him to be happy."

"Ah, true love," said Kristy. "Claudia, you're next."

"I'm sleeping," said Claudia.

"No, you're not," scolded Stacey. "Come on."

"Okay," said Claudia reluctantly. "I suppose I should resolve to do better at school. Your turn, Mal."

"I resolve to stop worrying about how I look in my brace. Might as well just grin and bear it, since I'm going to have it for a while. Now you, Jessi."

"I resolve to do a *ballotté*," she said.

"What's that?" asked Stacey.

"It's an advanced ballet jump. Madame Noelle says it's too difficult, and that I

38

should wait. But I want to, and I'm going to show her I can do it."

"Wow," said Stacey admiringly. "My resolution is to . . . um . . . stop wishing I could eat the foods I can't have. I just drive myself insane that way. Now you, Dawn."

The truth was, I had silently come up with a resolution. But for some reason, I didn't want to tell anyone. "I resolve to do something more interesting with my hair," I said quickly.

"Don't you dare! Your hair is gorgeous," Claudia said, half yawning.

"Thanks, but I think I could do with a change," I replied.

What I'd said was true, but only partly true. My silent resolution had been to get a boyfriend. And that would mean becoming more attractive to boys. I wasn't quite sure yet what I'd have to do. But whatever it was I was determined to do it.

4th CHAPTER

It snowed the day I went to sit for the Hills. Although I detest the cold weather, I do like snow. At least while it's falling. It makes everything so pretty and clean-looking. I feel as if I'm in one of those glass balls. You know, the kind that you shake, and snow swirls around a plastic house or snowman. I looked down at my black wool gloves and saw individual snowflakes that had fallen on them. They were beautiful.

So I was in a good mood as I rang the Hills' doorbell. After a minute or two, the door opened.

"Yes?" said Sarah Hill. She was a slim, pretty girl with large brown eyes. Her thin brown hair fell softly to the bottom of her long neck.

"Hi, Sarah," I said. "I'm Dawn. I'm here to babysit for you and your brother."

"Oh," she said, as if she hadn't known a

babysitter was coming. "Come in. I'll get my father."

As soon as she'd turned round and ran up the stairs, Sarah dropped her ladylike manner. "Dad!" she bellowed, disappearing down the hall. "Did you hire a babysitter?"

The Hills' house was modern with an unusual layout. As you walked in the front door, you entered a small hall. To the left was a staircase leading upstairs. To the right was another staircase leading down. From where I stood in the front hall, I could see the kitchen at the top of the stairs on the left.

In a minute, Mr Hill came to the upstairs landing. He was a very tall man with broad shoulders. He was almost bald. If it weren't for some brown hair on the sides, he would have reminded me of Mr Clean. (He didn't have an earring like Mr Clean, but you get the idea.)

"Hello," he said. "Your name is Dawn, right?"

"Right," I replied.

"Harold Hill." When I reached the top of the stairs he shook my hand. His hands were huge.

Standing in the kitchen, looking at us, was Norman Hill. He had short wispy, blond hair and bright blue eyes. And he was fat. (I don't mean to be unkind. There's just no other way to say it. He wasn't stout. He wasn't husky or stocky or pudgy. He was fat.) "Hi," I greeted him. "You must be Norman. I'm Dawn."

His face lit up when he smiled at me. "I didn't know you were coming," he said pleasantly.

Mr Hill opened the coat cupboard in the hall and began to pull on a red ski jacket. "Yes, that's my fault," he said. "I forgot to mention to the kids that I had to go out. I'm a computer systems consultant. I work here at home. It seems everyone is having computer problems today. I've been on the phone since this morning. Now I have to see a potential new client."

Stepping into the kitchen, Mr Hill grabbed a long yellow pad from the worktop. He ruffled Norman's wispy hair. "See ya, sport," he said, heading down the stairs.

"Wait! Wait!" I called. "Where are you going to be in case I need you?"

Mr Hill took his wallet from his back pocket. He dug through it until he found the business card he wanted. "Here," he said, handing it to me. "Here's where I'll be. My wife will be home before me, at about seven, seven-thirty."

"Do Norman and Sarah get supper or anything?" I asked.

With a quick movement, Mr Hill checked his watch. I suppose he was running late.

42

"No. Michelle, my wife, will feed them when she comes in. Anything else?"

"Do the kids get any medicine? Are they allergic to anything? Is there anything else I should know about them?"

"Nope, not a thing," he said, as he turned and headed out of the door. I wondered if he was always in such a hurry.

"So, Norman," I said, as I hung up my coat. "I suppose you weren't expecting me. Who used to babysit for you?"

"Our nanna," said Norman. "But she died."

"Oh, I'm sorry," I said. "How long ago?"

Norman wrinkled his brow in thought. "About a month or two. It was really sad. I miss her."

"I bet you do," I said. I felt bad about bringing up the subject. But Norman seemed to take it well enough.

"What do you usually do about this time?" I asked. "Do you have homework? Do you want to go outside and play in the snow?"

Again, Norman wrinkled his brow. "I think I'll do homework," he said, heading down the hall to his room. "I don't have a lot to do. I'll be right out."

Norman went to the room at the far end of the hall and shut the door. Just then Sarah's bedroom door opened. "Would you

43

like to see my room?" she asked, poking her head out.

"Okay," I said, as I walked towards her. Sarah's room was beautiful. The yellow flowered curtains matched the ruffled bedspread and the cover on her bedside table. Pictures of kittens decorated the walls. A gorgeous white desk sat in a corner.

But the room was a mess.

It looked like my mother's room might have looked when she was a girl.

Clothes were dumped on the desk chair and the bedposts. Books and Barbie clothes were all over the floor. Scraps of looseleaf paper with drawings scrawled across them were scattered everywhere. I didn't know where to sit.

"I'm getting new curtains and a new bedspread," she informed me. "They're going to be decorated with rainbows. I love rainbows, don't you?"

"Rainbows are pretty," I agreed.

"They're fun to draw. I love to draw. Do you?"

"I like it, but I'm not that great at it," I told her. "Do you have any homework?" I asked. "Norman is doing his at the moment."

Sarah's hands went to her hips. "First of all," she said in her grown-up voice, "I always do my homework as soon as I get home from school. So does Norman. It's my father's rule. Norman is not doing his homework now. Come on, I'll show you."

She walked past me, out of the bedroom door and down the hall. "It's okay," I said, stepping into the hall after her. "Maybe he just wants a bit of time to himself. Why don't we leave him alone?"

"Oh, no," Sarah replied firmly. "I know what he's doing. And he's not allowed to. My mother told me to make sure he doesn't." Without knocking, Sarah pushed her way into Norman's room.

I wasn't sure what to do. I didn't want to charge in on Norman. So I stayed in the hall.

"Dawn! Dawn!" Sarah called. "I told you he was doing it."

I thought I'd better see what was happening. Coming to Norman's door, I looked inside. Norman was sitting on the floor, surrounded by opened chocolate and cake wrappers. There was a smear of chocolate cupcake filling across his cheek.

"Leave me alone!" mumbled Norman, through a mouthful of chocolate. He looked at me quickly, and a pink blush swept across his face.

"Norman, why don't you clear up those wrappers and we'll play a board game or something," I suggested.

"Okay," he said, gulping down the last of the cupcake.

"Where did you hide the rest?" Sarah

45

demanded, as she looked around Norman's room. I noticed that Norman's room was as neat as a pin. He and Sarah appeared to be opposites in every way.

"Where is it, Norman?" Sarah asked again.

"There is no more," said Norman stubbornly.

Sarah turned to me. "Norman hides food in his room. We don't even know where he gets it. My mother told me that if I see it I should get rid of it. It's for his own good. Look at him. He's huge!"

I wanted to die. So I could imagine how Norman felt. I decided to distract Sarah. "Sarah, do you happen to have the video of *The Little Mermaid*?" I asked. (I had a feeling she probably did.)

"Of course. Why?" Sarah asked.

"It's my favourite film," I said. "I'd love to see it again. Do you think you could put it on for me?"

"*The Little Mermaid* is my favourite film, too!" Sarah cried, as if this were the most amazing coincidence on earth. As I'd hoped, she forgot about Norman and grabbed my hand. "Come on," she said, pulling me out of the room.

"Norman," I said, "do you want to see the video?"

"I suppose so." He shrugged.

The TV and VCR were in the large living room, at the opposite end of the hall. Sarah popped in the video and stretched out on the rug in front of the TV. Norman joined me on the sofa. "This is one of the most wonderful films ever made," Sarah said to me, not taking her eyes off the opening credits. "I know every song off by heart."

In minutes, Sarah was completely absorbed in the film. The only time she spoke was to sing along with the songs. Although I've seen *The Little Mermaid* quite a few times, I never get tired of it, either.

Norman, unfortunately, didn't feel the same way.

While Sarah sang along with the film, Norman poked my arm. I looked to see what he wanted. He had pulled a handful of toffees from his pocket. "Want one?" he whispered.

"No, thanks," I whispered back. "Why don't you wait until after supper?"

"All right," Norman agreed. But the next time I looked at him, he was chewing on a toffee. I don't know how he managed it. Each time I looked at him, he was chewing. I never saw him take out a sweet or unwrap it. This kid was fast.

Once I glanced at him quickly and saw him pop something into his mouth. Our eyes met. He looked at me and smiled. He didn't start chewing until I'd looked away again. Norman was obviously a skilful secret eater.

Towards the end of the film (the part in which it seems as though Ursula the Sea Witch might win), I noticed Norman wasn't sitting beside me any more. Quietly I got up and walked to the kitchen, which was just off the living room.

Norman was at the table, eating a peanut butter and jam sandwich. Beside the sandwich sat five toffees and a tall glass of milk. "You're going to spoil your appetite for supper," I warned him gently.

"We won't eat for a while," Norman protested. "Not until eight o'clock."

That did seem late. But how could he be hungry after eating all that cake and chocolate?

Just then, I was distracted by the sound of the doorbell ringing. When I got to the door, Sarah was already there. A girl her age stood on the front step. "Can I go out and play with Elizabeth?" Sarah asked. "She lives next door."

"I suppose that's okay," I agreed. "Don't leave the garden, though."

Sarah ran to get her coat. Elizabeth and I followed her. We stood together in the kitchen, waiting for Sarah. "Hiya, Normy," said Elizabeth, who was a small girl with red curls. "Eating again, huh?"

Elizabeth looked at me. "Guess what they call him at school. Enormous Hill! Isn't that funny?"

"No, I don't think it's funny," I replied.

"What's not funny?" asked Sarah, coming into the kitchen.

"Enormous Hill," Elizabeth told her. "It is so funny. You see, they say Enormous instead of Norman because it sounds like Norman, and since Norman is enormous and his last name is Hill they call him—"

"I realized that," I cut her off. "I just don't think it's funny."

Elizabeth looked at me as if I had no sense of humour. Sarah shot a disapproving look at Norman. "Stop eating!" she shouted.

In response, Norman took his sandwich and walked off to the living room. "You're not allowed to eat in there!" Sarah called after him.

Norman didn't reply. "He isn't supposed to eat in there," Sarah told me. "It's my mother's rule."

"I'll deal with it," I told her. "You and Elizabeth go outside and play."

I was relieved when I heard the door slam. Poor Norman. Not only was his sister a tyrant, her friend was a bully!

Enormous Hill. What a horrible name. That's one thing I don't understand about kids. Why are they so cruel sometimes?

"Sarah's gone," I said, as I walked into the living room. "Why don't you take that sandwich back to the kitchen?" I really didn't have to worry at that point. Norman had downed most of the sandwich already.

He got up from the sofa and brought his plate back to the kitchen. I was surprised to see him put back his jars, wipe the table, and place his dish in the dishwasher. Most boys his age aren't that neat. But then I wondered if it was more than being neat. Maybe it was also another way to hide the fact that he'd been eating.

When that was done, Norman sat down and started on his toffees. "Sarah and Elizabeth were pretty hard on you," I said, settling myself beside him. "Are you okay?"

"I'm used to it," said Norman, as he popped a toffee into his mouth. "It's not just Sarah. It's everybody. My whole family bugs me about my weight."

"What do they do?" I asked.

"My mother is always taking me to see these doctors. At first my parents thought something was the matter with my glands. They thought that was why I'm fat. But the doctors said no. I just eat too much."

"What did the doctors say to do?"

"They gave me all these yucky diets to go on," Norman said, making a face. "My mother cooks stuff like brown rice and fish. Really gross stuff."

"I like brown rice," I said.

"Then you're weird," Norman replied. "That stuff's horrible. Guess where my parents are sending me this summer."

"Where?" I asked.

"To Fat Camp," he said grimly.

"You mean a weight reduction camp?"

"Yup. Fat Camp."

"Maybe it will help," I suggested.

Norman shook his head. "I don't want to go to camp. It's for eight weeks. I don't want to go away for the whole summer. I'm not going. They can't make me."

"Have you told your parents how you feel?"

"Yeah," Norman replied. "They said if I lose twenty pounds, I don't have to go."

"Then there's the solution!" I said. "You have to stick to a diet and lose twenty pounds."

Norman sighed and glumly propped his chin in his hands. "I like eating. I don't want to stop eating. I get sick of everyone telling me what to do."

Just then, a snowball hit the kitchen window. I got up and looked outside. In the back garden Sarah and Elizabeth had built a snowman. It had only two sections. A small head with stones forming the features of his face, and a big bottom. The snowman was all out of proportion. The body was too big for the head.

Sarah and Elizabeth saw me looking. Sarah fiddled with her mitten. There was a guilty look on her face.

Then I saw why.

Elizabeth was laughing and pointing with a stick to the snow in front of the snowman. In the snow were written the words, Enormous Hill.

5th CHAPTER

When I walked through my front door that evening, I was feeling pretty miserable. I wasn't ill or anything, just miserable.

I felt so sorry for Norman Hill. Before I could stop him, he'd come to the window and looked out at the fat snowman. You should have seen his face. It would have broken your heart.

"They're just trying to wind you up, Norman," I said.

"It's okay," he replied. "I'm used to it."

Later, when I looked out of the window again, the snowman was smashed. I wondered if Sarah had done it. Was she feeling guilty? Maybe she just didn't want to get into trouble.

Poor Norman. He didn't even get a break when his mother came home. Mrs Hill is a small, thin woman. Sarah looks exactly like her. The minute she walked through the door, Sarah told her mother that Norman had been eating in his room. "And he's been eating all day long," Sarah added, as she followed her mother up the stairs.

"Is that true?" Mrs Hill asked me, before even saying hello. (So far, Mr and Mrs Hill were not winning any popularity votes with me.)

Norman and I were sitting at the kitchen table. He was showing me a book he'd just got. It was *The Marvel Encyclopaedia of Super Heroes*. I've never been big on super heroes, but Norman made it seem quite interesting.

"He did have a few snacks," I admitted to Mrs Hill. (Luckily, Norman wasn't eating at the moment.) "But I wouldn't say he was eating all day long," I added quickly.

"He was too!" Sarah insisted.

Mrs Hill just sighed as she opened the fridge and stared into it wearily. She pulled out a bowl of tuna salad. Taking a clean plate from the dishwasher, she plopped a large spoonful of the salad on it. "Here's your supper Norman," she said, sticking a fork into the mound of tuna and placing it in front of him. "How was your day, sweetheart?"

"All right, I suppose. I had fun with Dawn," he answered.

"I'm glad," she told him with a small smile, though she didn't ask what we had done or anything else. Mrs Hill paid me as I put on my coat. "You did a great job," she said, walking me to the door. "Just don't let Norman eat so much next time you come."

I was still thinking about the Hills as I stood at our cooker and cooked a soyabean burger. The rest of my family had already eaten supper. Mum and Richard were at a PTA meeting. Jeff had gone back to California, and Mary Anne was studying at Logan's.

It was odd having the house so empty and quiet. Odd but nice. I wouldn't want to be alone all the time, but I like it once in a while.

I wasn't alone for long, though. The front door slammed, and Mary Anne came bounding into the kitchen. Her eyes were lit up with excitement. "We have an official date," she told me. "I'm going to mark it on the calendar." She went to the wall calendar and wrote LBA in the box for January the thirteenth. Then she drew a big star around the letters.

"What's LBA?" I asked as I took my burger to the table.

"Lewis Bruno arrives!" she said brightly. "I was there when he phoned. I even spoke to him. Oh, Dawn, he seems so nice! He sounds just like Logan. He has that same cute accent, and even his voice is the same. It's unbelievable. You're going to like Lewis so much."

Suddenly a lump of soyabean burger got stuck in my throat.

I stood up and started coughing. Mary Anne hopped around me anxiously. "Are you okay?"

"Water," I spluttered.

Quickly, Mary Anne got me some. In a minute I was okay.

"Was it something I said?" Mary Anne asked.

"Maybe. January the thirteenth is just a week from today. I won't be ready by then."

"Ready?" Mary Anne asked. "What do you have to do?"

"Oh, um, nothing," I stammered. "I don't know why I said that."

Mary Anne looked confused. I hadn't told her, or anyone, about my plan to make myself more attractive to boys. I'd decided Lewis would be my test case. If I could make him like me—I mean *really* like me—then I would know what to do with boys in general.

I should have been able to tell this to Mary Anne. You can usually tell her just about anything, and she tries to understand. But somehow I felt awkward about it.

To be honest, I was a bit embarrassed. I'd always thought Mary Anne looked up to me. (At least a little.) I thought she saw me as secure and confident. I didn't want to shatter her image of me as an individualist.

Boy, was I wrong.

As it turned out, I wasn't the only one who thought I could do with a make-over. Mary Anne thought so, too!

I didn't discover this until that evening. I'd gone up to my room with a pile of fashion magazines. I'd borrowed them from Stacey the week before. I'm usually not terribly interested in that stuff. This was why I still hadn't got around to looking through them. But there was no time left. Lewis was coming in a week. I had to get going on my make-over—and fast.

As I flicked through the magazines, I tried to find ways to add some pizzazz to my looks. According to the first magazine I skimmed through, my clothes were far too baggy. I like wearing loose clothing because it's comfortable. This was apparently all wrong. There were no baggy clothes in the magazine.

Next I realized I would need more make-up. The magazines tell you what to wear. (Boy, do they tell you. It sounds so complicated! They should give college courses on applying make-up. Highlighter along the brow bone and upper temples. Three different shades of eye-shadow for different "quadrants" of your eye. Lip "fixer", then lip liner, then lipstick, then lip gloss. It made my algebra assignments seem easy.)

As I read an article called "Fixing Facial Flaws," Mary Anne came into the room. "What are you doing?" she asked.

"Nothing," I replied.

Mary Anne took the magazine from my lap. "Wow! Dawn, I've never seen you look through something like this. What's up?"

"I was just curious," I said.

Mary Anne sat on the edge of my bed and flipped through the pages. She seemed to be searching for something in particular. "I was looking through this issue at Stacey's house, and I saw an outfit and a hairstyle that would be great on you," she said excitedly. "The girl even looks like you. I didn't mention it because I thought you might think it was stupid. But since you don't, I'll show you."

Mary Anne found the page. "Here, what do you think?" she asked, as she handed me back the magazine. It was a full-colour picture of a girl standing on some rocks overlooking the ocean. Her hair was long and blonde like mine. But it was super wavy. Probably permed. She wore a light blue unitard that reached just below her calves. Over the unitard was a very short (the caption said "bolero-style") faded blue denim jacket with all sorts of clunky pins on the top pockets.

Her face was made up a little more heavily than some of the other models in the magazine. She seemed to have on more eye make-up. The make-up went with her expression. It was kind of tough and serious.

58

"I wonder how I'd look with a perm," I considered.

"We could find out," said Mary Anne. "We'll set it with electric rollers. Of course, it won't be permanent, but you'll get the idea."

"Do we have electric rollers?" I asked.

"Your mum does. Want me to get them?"

"Sure. Why not?" I said, trying to sound casual. It was as if Mary Anne were reading my mind.

Mary Anne ran out of the room. In a moment she came back with electric rollers, a curling iron, and a clear plastic box loaded with make-up. I'd forgotten Mum even had all this stuff. These days she just blow-dried her hair and used a little eye make-up and lipstick.

I sat on the bed, and Mary Anne plugged in the rollers and the curling iron. We had to wait for them to warm up. "Let's see how you'd look with some make-up," she suggested.

"I don't know much about putting it on," I admitted.

"I'll do it," Mary Anne volunteered. She flicked through the same magazine once more. "Here's a step-by-step make-over. It tells you exactly what to do. I'm sure I can follow the directions."

Pretty soon the curlers were warmed up. Mary Anne used all of them, and even that wasn't enough to curl my hair. "That's why I brought in the curling iron," she explained. "I'll curl up the bottom while the top is baking."

Once the bottom was curled and the top rollers were out, I looked as though I had three times as much hair. It was hilarious. "I look like Dolly Parton!" I cried, half laughing, half worrying.

"We haven't combed it yet," said Mary Anne. "First let's put on the make-up." Mary Anne piled all the curls on top of my head. Then she began sorting through Mum's make-up box.

"Okay, we'll start with some foundation," she said, opening the bottle of flesh-toned liquid. Mary Anne put the foundation on with a steady hand. I was surprised at how assured she seemed. Especially since she doesn't wear much make-up herself.

"How did you get so good at this?" I asked.

"I'm just doing what they say in the magazine," she explained, as she brushed blusher on my cheeks. "I think it must be easier to make up someone else than to make up yourself." She worked a bit longer, putting on eye make-up and lipstick. "Make-up's done," she announced, blotting my lips with a tissue.

Then Mary Anne told me to put my head between my knees and brush out my hair. As I did that, she sprayed the underside of my hair with small blasts from a can of hair spray. "Stacey told me about this," she explained. "It's supposed to give your hair volume."

When I finally stood in front of the mirror, I was stunned. Mary Anne was a genius! I did look like the girl in the magazine. (Pretty close, anyway.)

"Lewis is going to fall madly in love when he sees you," Mary Anne commented.

"You really think so?" I asked, staring into the mirror. "Do you really think Lewis will like me like this?"

"He's got to. You're a knockout," said Mary Anne.

Suddenly I had an idea. "I want to send him a picture of me the way I look right now. That way he won't be too surprised when we meet."

"Great idea," Mary Anne agreed. "I'll get the camera." While she was gone, I changed clothes. I pulled off my big sweat shirt. But I didn't know what else to put on.

I wanted something really daring. The kind of thing I didn't own. I'd seen lots of off-the-shoulder tops in the magazines. I didn't have one, of course—but it was easy to create one.

"What are you doing?" Mary Anne said, gasping, as she came back into the room.

I was cutting a red long-sleeved T-shirt half way down the front. "You'll see," I told her. I put on the T-shirt, tucking in both sides of the front. "*Ta-da!*" I sang, slipping the shoulders down my arms.

"You look great," Mary Anne said. "I know! Toss your hair over one shoulder so your earrings show."

I stood by our bedroom window and did what she said. Mary Anne aimed the camera at me. "Say cheese!"

At first, I started to smile. Then I stopped myself. Instead, I puffed out my lower lip and glared into the camera.

"What kind of face is that?" Mary Anne asked, lowering the camera.

"I'm trying to look like the girl in the magazine," I explained. "You know, mysterious and alluring."

"It might work," Mary Anne agreed. She raised the camera again and snapped the picture. In a few minutes the photo was developed. I couldn't believe it. It was as if I were seeing a picture of someone else.

"You really should be a model," Mary Anne commented, as she looked at the photo.

I took it from her. "Lewis Bruno, look out," I said. "Here comes the new Dawn."

6th CHAPTER

Friday

Yesterday afternoon I sat for Sarah and Norman Hill. I fell so sory for Norman. A bunch of kids picked on him all the way home from school. He felt terible when he came in. Then Sarah started bugging him. She was really mean.

But you know what I unerstand how Sarah feels. I think she is just fristraded with Norman. She wants him to lose wate, but he keeps eating and eating (and eating and eating and eating).

I'm glad I can eat lots of junk food and not gane wate. I wonder if I could stop if I started to get fat. It probibly wuldn't be easy. Poor Norman.

Claudia got the job at the Hills' house during a Wednesday afternoon BSC meeting. Stacey picked up the phone and talked to Mr Hill. He wanted someone for Thursday at three-thirty. Mr Hill had a new, important client. He had lots of meetings scheduled. He said he'd be calling regularly in the next couple of weeks. Claud took the job, since she was the only one of us who was free.

I had told her about my experiences with Sarah and Norman, so she was prepared. But I still think she was glad that Norman was at his after-school programme when she arrived at his house. For one thing, it meant she wouldn't have to stop Sarah from picking on Norman. I'd warned Claud about that.

Do you want to hear something interesting? Every sitter has a slightly different reaction to the kids we sit for. For example, I really didn't like Sarah Hill all that much. But Claud ended up liking her a lot.

It might be because they are both artistic. And maybe because Claud understands how it feels to have a brother or sister who is sort of odd. Claud's sister, Janine, isn't fat, but she *is* a little odd. She's a genius. And she can be extremely annoying. She's always telling you when you've made a mistake. Janine is not very popular. (I think maybe Claud does badly at school because she doesn't want to be *anything* like Janine.)

Anyway, as I said, Claud and Sarah really hit it off.

Claud was giving Sarah a drawing lesson when something awful happened. (I'm glad I wasn't there to see this.) Claudia and Sarah stopped what they were doing, because they heard the sound of shouting outside. "Enormous Hill! Oink! Oink! Hey, Enormous Hill!"

When Claud reached the front door, a snowball slammed right into the glass. Luckily it didn't break. The kids were throwing snowballs at Norman. As soon as they saw Claud, they turned and ran. Cowards.

"Are you all right?" asked Claud, brushing snow off Norman's hat as he came through the door. His head was down and his eyes were brimming with tears. He didn't say anything, just walked straight up to the kitchen.

"Hey, remember you're on a diet!" Sarah called, when she heard a cabinet door open.

"Take it easy," Claud told her. "He's just had a pretty awful experience."

Sarah looked up at her. "It's for his own good. My mother says so. I know he's eating something bad now."

Sure enough, Norman had opened a packet of biscuits. Sarah snatched the packet from him. "Mum told me to take these away from you."

Norman's face grew red with anger. He didn't say a word, though. He just stormed off to his bedroom.

At that moment, the doorbell rang. Sarah ran to answer it. It was Elizabeth, from next door. "Can I go outside for a while?" Sarah called to Claud. "I'll stay in our garden."

"Of course," Claud answered.

After Sarah left, Claud knocked on Norman's door. "Norman, can I come in?" she asked.

She heard movement inside, but got no answer. "Norman," she tried again. "Are you okay?"

Still no answer.

Claud decided she would probably leave him alone for a while. She went back to the living room and started to browse through some art magazines. (Mrs Hill is an agent for illustrators. She has tons of art books and magazines in the house, so Claud was in heaven.) About half an hour later, she heard Norman's door creak open.

Pretending she was still reading, Claud waited to see what he would do. She wasn't surprised that he tiptoed into the kitchen. Like a hungry mouse, Norman was rustling around in the kitchen once again.

Claud got up and tiptoed to the kitchen doorway. Norman was so intent on wolfing down some cookies he'd found that he didn't notice her. "Norman," Claud said after a moment.

Norman nearly jumped off his chair. He began stuffing the cookies back into the bag.

"Relax. It's okay," said Claud, sitting down beside him. "I won't tell on you. I'm Claudia, by the way."

"Hi," he mumbled through a mouthful of cookies. "Where's Dawn?"

Claud explained to him how the BSC worked. He didn't look too pleased. Some kids like the variety of sitters. Others would rather have the same one all the time.

Norman continued eating cookies until Claud felt that she had to say something. "They aren't going to help your diet much."

"It's not *my* diet," Norman replied.

"What do you mean?" Claud asked, puzzled.

"It's my parents' diet. They talked to the doctor. They decided I should go on it. So it's *their* diet."

"But they're doing it for you," Claud pointed out.

"No, they're not," Norman disagreed, as he took another cookie. "They're doing it for them. They don't want to have a fat son."

"Do *you* want to be heavy?" Claud pressed gently.

Norman shrugged. "I don't like being

fat, but I like eating. If I feel sad, eating makes me feel happy."

"Do you feel sad a lot?" asked Claud.

"Sometimes," Norman admitted. "I don't feel sad when I'm eating, though."

"Maybe you wouldn't feel sad if you lost some weight," Claud suggested. "You might feel happier if the kids didn't pick on you and call you names."

"I don't care about them. I have other friends," Norman insisted. "I have a friend at school called Teddy. And I have a girlfriend."

"You do?" said Claud, trying hard not to sound surprised.

Norman took a deep gulp of milk, then he nodded. "Yeah. Brittany. She's my pen pal. I think I'll write to her now." Stuffing five more cookies into his pockets, Norman headed out of the kitchen to his room.

With a sigh, Claud returned to the living room and her magazines. Only this time, she couldn't concentrate on them. She had to find some way to get through to Norman. Somebody had to. Otherwise he was just going to keep getting fatter and more miserable.

About half an hour later, the phone rang. "Hi, this is Teddy," said a young voice on the other end. "Is Norman there?"

"I'll get him," said Claud, glad there really was a Teddy. "Norman," she called, as she leaned down the hall to his room. "Phone for you. It's Teddy."

Norman's door opened. He came out, holding a green spiral bound notebook. "Okay, thanks," he said, passing her in the hall. "I told you I had a friend."

As he headed for the kitchen phone, a piece of paper fluttered from his notebook. Claud picked it up. It appeared to be a draft of a letter to his pen pal. Well, what do you know, thought Claud. There really is a Teddy and there really is a pen pal.

Maybe Claud shouldn't have read Norman's letter, but she did. She was hoping it might help her understand Norman better. "Dear Brittany," it said. "Today was another awesome day for me. I managed to clobber some school bullies, and good. They were picking on this kid at school. He's a totally amazing kid, just slightly heavy. That's why they pick on him. About ten bullies surrounded him. They were the gooniest kids in the whole school— and the ugliest. And they were big and mean. Everyone else is afraid of them. I'm not. I grabbed one of them and karate-chopped him. His friend tried to get me, but I hit him with my flying judo kick. Every-one was cheering. Kids at school were yelling, 'Norman! Norman! Go! Go! Go!' Two boys came at me at once. I clunked their heads together. That made the rest of them run away.

"That was my day. How was yours? Thanks for the picture you sent. You are very pretty. I don't have any pictures of myself. But I'll send you one as soon as my mother's camera is fixed. I keep reminding her to fix it, but she keeps forgetting."

Claud put the letter back in Norman's room. She dropped it on his floor so he wouldn't know she'd read it. On his desk was a sheet of recent wallet-sized pictures of Norman. They looked like his school pictures.

Somehow Claud was pretty sure that Brittany was never going to see one of them, or any other picture of her pen pal.

7th CHAPTER

Time was running out. Less than a week remained before Lewis arrived. I'd sent him the picture Mary Anne took of "the new Dawn." Mary Anne also took a second picture in a slightly different pose. I kept that one.

Funny about the second picture. I couldn't stop looking at it. I stuck it in my wallet and looked at it a lot. Something about the photo fascinated me. It was as if it were of me—but not me.

The reason hit me during a physics lesson on Monday afternoon. I'd stuck the photo in my textbook and was gazing down at it. (I'd already finished the section we were supposed to be reading. I read pretty fast.) I suddenly realized that this was a picture of the person I was going to become. Like a glimpse into the future.

And it wasn't all about looks, either.

Okay, that was a big part of it. But it was also about attitude. There was something about not smiling for the camera that made everything clear to me. The old Dawn was always so eager to make people happy. Always pleasant and polite. The Dawn in the picture didn't care. The new Dawn was cool.

At that moment, I had a chance to try out my new attitude. Miss Harris, my science teacher, told us to stop reading. "Okay, quick test," she said. She does this pretty regularly. You get two points on your next test mark if you answer her questions correctly. You lose two points if you don't. She calls on people at random.

"Dawn," she said. "Name two common forms of igneous rock."

Physics is not my favourite subject. But I could answer that one. Granite and basalt. It was right in the text.

I opened my mouth to speak, but something stopped me. I didn't feel like being Agreeable Dawn, Good Pupil. Cool kids didn't sit up straight and answer all the teacher's questions. They slouched and stared into space as if everything were a bore.

"Heavy metal and pop," I answered, tossing my hair over my shoulder.

My teacher looked confused, then shocked.

She couldn't have been more shocked

than I was. I couldn't believe I had actually said that!

A ripple of low laughter swept through the class. A cute boy named Bill Torrance looked over at me and smiled. He'd never done that before. It was working!

"Very amusing, Dawn," said Miss Harris. "But I wasn't talking about rock and roll. I was talking about igneous rock."

"Is that a new group?" I asked boldly.

The class laughed again. It was great. They were seeing me in a new light.

So was Miss Harris. She didn't look happy, though. "I take it you don't know the answer," she said calmly.

"No, I don't," I lied.

Miss Harris made a mark in her grade book and then called on someone else. She was still asking questions when I noticed a note being passed my way.

Inside the note was a drawing of a rock band. The members had rocks for heads. On top was written "Igneous Rock! Good one, Dawn!" It was from Sue Archer, a very cool girl in my class. She'd never sent me a note before. Being cool was easier than I'd thought.

From that moment on, there was no stopping me. It was Project New Dawn all the way!

The new me needed time the next morning to put on make-up, do my hair, and choose what clothes to wear. I needed so much extra time that I missed the bus. (Was Mum ever angry when she had to drive me to school. She would have been even angrier if she'd seen that I'd purposely ripped my new jeans. But I wore a long coat, so she never knew.)

Clothing was the biggest problem. My clothes were all wrong. I couldn't find anything to wear. I had to spend Tuesday evening altering them.

"Have you gone nuts?" Mary Anne gasped, when she saw what I was doing to my wardrobe. A pile of clothes were strewn over my bed. I was completely revamping everything with the help of Mum's sewing kit and a pair of sharp scissors.

All my jeans needed to be taken in. (I ripped one more pair above the knee and left one pair unripped.) I made several off-the-shoulder tops. I even created a miniskirt out of a pair of grey tracksuit bottoms. I cut off the legs, opened the inside seams, and then patched up the gaps with some flowered material. (It was left over from a flowered T-shirt I'd cut up.)

"That's quite nice," said Mary Anne, holding up the grey skirt. "You should get Claudia to help you."

"Nah," I disagreed. "Claud has a unique style. I want to create my *own* style."

"Wow," Mary Anne murmured. "I know we experimented with a new look, but you're going all out. How come? Is it because of Lewis?"

"Not really," I replied. "It's just time for a change, that's all." I was going to tell her why I felt I needed a new image. That it wasn't just because of Lewis. It was because I was a flop with boys altogether. But I'd noticed that cool kids don't talk a lot. They don't explain everything they're thinking and feeling. Cool kids just go ahead and do what they want to do.

"Maybe it is time," Mary Anne agreed.

Mary Anne was really surprising me. Was she just being supportive? Or had she been thinking something was wrong with me all along? I had expected a *little* argument from her. A little "Dawn, you're fine the way you are." I didn't know if I was glad or annoyed that she didn't say that.

I take that back. I did know. I felt that I *should* be glad. But deep down I was annoyed.

My friends had different reactions to my new appearance.

"You look strange," Kristy said. (I more or less expected that from her.)

"You don't need so much blusher," Stacey advised me.

Claudia's reaction took me by surprise. "The look is all wrong for you," she said. "It's not who you are." Can you imagine Claud—of all people—saying that? I just shrugged. (Cool kids shrug a lot.) But inside

I was steaming. I suppose Claudia thought it was okay for her and Stacey to be stylish and cute, but not me. No. I was just plain, wholesome Dawn, and I was supposed to stay that way.

I decided she might even be jealous. She might not want anyone looking more "unique" than she did herself.

So, by the time of our Wednesday afternoon BSC meeting, I was pretty angry with Claudia. I slumped on her bed, chewing hard on a wad of pink bubble gum. (It was sugarless.)

"I've never seen you chew gum before," Stacey observed.

"There's a first time for everything," I replied.

"Can you blow a bubble?" asked Mal from her spot on the floor.

I shook my head. Believe it or not, this *was* the first piece of bubble gum I'd ever chewed.

"Do you have another piece?" she asked me.

I took one from my back pocket and gave it to her. She quickly chewed it, then blew a giant bubble. "You flatten it down, then stick your tongue into it and blow," she instructed me.

I tried and got a small bubble going.

Kristy started the meeting. She talked about organizing a pizza party next Monday afternoon. Everyone would meet at a pizza

76

parlour with their babysitting charges. It was a good idea, but there were millions of tiny problems. Jessi would be sitting for a kid who was allergic to tomato sauce. Mary Anne wasn't sure she could keep all three Barrett kids under control in the pizzeria. Claud was sitting for a family with a very temperamental baby. Stacey would be sitting for the Hills that day. From what she'd heard, she didn't think the Hills would want Norman eating pizza.

Right from the start, I could tell the plan wasn't going to work. Also, I didn't much care, since I wasn't sitting that afternoon. I was more interested in perfecting my bubble-blowing technique. *Crack!* a small one popped.

Kristy had been talking. She shot me a Look. I wasn't in the mood for Kristy's big-boss attitude. I blew another bubble. This one grew really big. *Crack!* It popped even more loudly than the one before.

"Do you mind?" Kristy snapped.

"Calm down," I replied. "It's just a bubble. It's not as though I set off a firecracker or something."

"Can I ask you a question?" said Kristy angrily. "What is it with you the last few days? You're acting totally weirdly."

"I am not," I protested.

"Yes, you are," Claudia jumped in. "You seem like someone else."

"You do," agreed Stacey.

This was just great! My friends were ganging up on me. "What law says I always have to be the same?" I asked them. "When Mary Anne changed her hair and clothes, nobody jumped all over her."

Everyone looked at Mary Anne.

"It's not the same," said Kristy.

"Why not?" I challenged.

"Because Mary Anne didn't start *acting* differently," Claudia remarked.

"You lot are crazy," I insisted. "I'm not acting differently. You just think so because I look a little different. *Excuse me* for blowing bubbles, all right? I won't blow another one as long as I live."

"Are you doing this because of Lewis?" Stacey asked.

"In a way yes, and in a way no," I said truthfully.

"That really answers the question," Kristy scoffed.

Stacey let Kristy's remark pass. "Because if you are, maybe you shouldn't. Just be yourself.

"Look," I said, sitting forward. "It's easy for you to talk. Boys *like* you. They don't like me when I'm myself. I have to change. That's how I feel. So please don't bug me about it any more."

"I know what Dawn means," Mary Anne said loyally. "Everyone should be allowed to change. I mean, we're only thirteen.

None of us will stay exactly as we are for the rest of our lives."

"I suppose so," Stacey grumbled.

"I liked you better the way you were before," Claud insisted, looking at me critically.

"Let's get back to the meeting," said Kristy irritably. "So, okay, my great pizza party idea looks like a washout . . ."

Just then the phone rang. It was Dr Johanssen. Stacey took the job of sitting for eight-year-old Charlotte. Everyone began talking about what a great kid Charlotte is, but I really wasn't listening. I was furious with all of them except Mary Anne. I was only annoyed and confused by Mary Anne. (I wasn't angry with Jessi or Mal, either, since they hadn't said anything.) I wanted to get out of there and back to my room.

Finally the meeting ended. "Are you angry?" Mary Anne asked, as we walked across our lawn.

"No," I lied.

"You seem angry," she pressed.

"Well, maybe a little," I admitted, opening the front door. "Why can't they leave me alone?"

"Because they care about you."

"That's not why," I argued, as I pulled off my jacket. "They just want me to stay the same. At least you understand."

"I think I do," Mary Anne replied.

"Don't be angry with them. They'll get used to the new you."

Mary Anne disappeared into the kitchen, and I ran upstairs. I wanted to send Lewis one last piece of post before he arrived.

It was a postcard I'd bought recently. It showed the back of a big chair. All you saw were a woman's curvy legs hanging over the side. She wore red high heels.

"Dear Lewis," I wrote. "Dying to see you Friday night. Mary Anne said you have an extremely hunky voice. Can't wait to hear it whisper in my ear. Until then, Dawn."

Did I dare send it? The old Dawn wouldn't even have written it. The new Dawn stamped it and ran downstairs, out to the letterbox.

8th CHAPTER

There's one thing about New York City I can't get used to. It's how bright it is at night. The bridges, the buildings, the streets—they're so lit up you can hardly see the stars.

We weren't actually in the city. But we were right outside it. Mary Anne, Logan, and I sat in the back seat of the Brunos' big car as Mr Bruno drove towards La Guardia Airport. Lewis had tried to get a flight into our local airport but those flights were booked. It's easier to get a flight into La Guardia because more planes land there.

Logan and Mary Anne held hands throughout the whole journey. It made me feel a little weird to be sitting back there with them.

"I can't wait to see Lewis," said Logan.

"Thank goodness he's finally here,"

Mary Anne added. "The waiting was killing me."

Killing *her*! What about me? I felt as if I'd been waiting forever. The last week had been the longest one in my life!

"Be careful," said Mrs Bruno to her husband. "Take it slow. We have lots of time." It was eight o'clock. Lewis was coming in at 8:38, and we'd all be there to meet him.

"Please leave the driving to me," said Mr Bruno in a low voice. I didn't blame him for being aggravated. Mrs Bruno was a terrible back seat driver. I don't think she was used to being in city traffic.

Talk about bright. The airport was a blaze of lights. And people were everywhere. Airports always amaze me. So many people (not to mention so many jets) are going in so many different directions at once. It looks like mass confusion. Yet, for the most part, everyone gets where they're going.

"This is so exciting," said Mary Anne, as we followed Mr and Mrs Bruno down a long (bright) corridor to Gate 12. That was the gate Lewis would come through when he got off the plane. "Isn't it exciting, Dawn?"

"Oh, yeah, it is," I replied.

I really felt more sick than excited. I was so nervous, a knot had formed in the pit of my stomach. This was the big moment.

Lewis would step off that plane and we'd finally meet.

They say first impressions last. That's why I had done my best to make an unforgettable first expression. On Thursday afternoon I took all my babysitting money and went to Zingy's. It's this great shop that sells very trendy clothes. I didn't even take Mary Anne with me. I wanted to go by myself.

The salesperson at Zingy's had short maroon hair and four holes pierced in each ear. At first I was intimidated by her hair, but she turned out to be very nice. She helped me put together a great outfit, which was what I was wearing as we waited for Lewis.

Here's the outfit: black ballet slippers; black lace capri leggings; a short metallic silver skirt with all this crinoliny stuff underneath that made it stick out; a stretchy, tight, black-and-white-striped top with long sleeves. I'd bought six rubber bangle bracelets, and a new pair of feather earrings that reached down to my shoulders. (I wore both earrings in the two holes in my right ear. I put a pair of small black hoops in the two holes on the left.) This time I didn't set my hair; I piled it on top of my head, then made six plaits.

Mary Anne helped me put on my make-up. "Are you sure you want to wear that skirt?" she asked, as she gently lined my eyes.

"Yes! I bought it especially for tonight," I insisted.

"Okay, I was just asking," said Mary Anne.

When I came down the stairs, my mother was sitting on the sofa. She kept opening her mouth, as though she wanted to say something to me, and then closing it. In the end, all she said was, "Don't you need heavier socks? It's cold out."

"I'll be in the car," I told her.

So far, Mum was being very quiet about my new look. I knew she and Richard had talked about it. I passed their bedroom late one night. Their door was half open. They were speaking softly, but I heard Mum say, "It's just a phase. Let's be patient." I knew who they were talking about.

I was glad Mum felt that way. I hated to tell her this was no phase, but if she wanted to think it was, let her. It made my life easier.

So, thanks to Mum's phase theory, I got out of the house with my new look. Unfortunately, I wasn't a hundred per cent sure of myself. Part of me (the biggest part) thought I looked good that night. I mean, I would have looked good in a magazine. But I wasn't in a magazine. So I felt a little strange. You know. Maybe a bit overdone.

I didn't change anything, though. I knew

the old Dawn was just rising up inside me. The old Dawn was still alive and well. She was telling me to wash my face and put on something comfortable.

I couldn't listen to her.

Other boys hadn't liked the old Dawn. Why should Lewis? If I wanted him to like me, I had to stick to my plan and let the new Dawn shine through.

"There he is!" Logan cried suddenly.

A boy with short, wavy, dark hair strode out of the doorway along with the other arriving passengers. Lewis had told me in a letter that he was five feet, ten inches, but he looked taller. He was thin but not skinny. And a lot handsomer than he looked in his picture.

In a moment he spotted us. His face broke into this absolutely great smile—even better than the smile in his picture.

I'm not sure what love at first sight feels like. But I think that's what I felt right then. Lewis was even better than I'd expected. Mary Anne had been right, too. He had a great voice.

"Hi! Hi," he said as he hugged his aunt and uncle. He and Logan hugged, then they punched each other on the arms a little. "Man! I'm glad to see you!" Lewis told Logan.

"Me, too!" said Logan. "We are going to have a blast." Logan stood there smiling, then he remembered Mary Anne and me. "This is Mary Anne. And this is Dawn."

"Hi," I said a little shyly.

"Dawn, hi," said Lewis. He didn't give me his big, gorgeous smile. His mouth kind of quivered up into a small shaky one. "We meet at last."

"Yup," I said. (Real brilliant of me.)

"How was your flight, dear?" Mrs Bruno asked, putting her arm around Lewis.

"A little bumpy," he said. "But not bad."

Together, we headed back to the car. Lewis had only brought his flight bag so we didn't have to go to the baggage terminal. Soon we were on the motorway, driving back to Connecticut, with the city lights dimly flickering behind us. Logan, Mary Anne, Lewis, and I were squashed together in the back seat. Lewis was by the window, and I was between him and Mary Anne.

"I have a question, Lewis," said Mary Anne, happy and chirpy. "Is Dawn the way you pictured her?"

I wanted to die!

"Not really," he answered. He turned to me and smiled that quivery smile again. "You do look more like the second picture you sent. But I suppose I had a different idea of you. Do I seem the same to you?"

"Yeah," I answered. I couldn't say, "Oh, no, you're much dreamier than I expected!" Could I? Maybe I should have. That's the

86

kind of thing boys like to hear. I think. It just sounded too silly to say. Especially since he hadn't said anything like that about me.

I had a feeling I wasn't doing too well with Lewis.

Apparently Mary Anne had the same feeling.

No sooner had the Brunos dropped us off at our drive than she turned on me. "What is the matter with you?" she exploded.

"What do you mean?" I asked, heading for the house.

"I'm supposed to be the shy one!" she said, as she walked beside me. "All you said was, 'hi, yeah, no.' How about showing him a little personality?"

"I didn't know what to say," I grumbled. "He didn't like me, anyway. I could tell."

"Hi," said Richard, as we walked through the door. "How did it go?"

"Great!" said Mary Anne.

"Awful," I said at the same time.

"I see," said Richard, knitting his brow. I didn't feel like talking to him or anyone else. Throwing off my coat, I stormed up the stairs.

"Don't worry," I heard Mary Anne tell her father. "She'll be okay."

I was in my room, tearing off my clothing, when Mary Anne came in. "I'm sorry I yelled," she apologized. "You were just nervous. And I know you don't have much experience with boys. I shouldn't have shouted at you."

"Forget it, Mary Anne," I said, as I pulled off my lace leggings and threw them on the bed. "It was a stupid idea. He hates me. I told you he would. Boys hate me. That's just how it is."

"He doesn't hate you," said Mary Anne, picking up one of the fashion magazines from the desk. "How could he hate you? You didn't say anything for him to hate. You didn't say *anything*! That was the problem."

Mary Anne looked through the magazine until she found the article she wanted. Folding the pages back, she handed it to me. "I was looking at this last night," she said. "This is what you need to read."

I read the title. " 'You-Directed Conversation.' "

"It's all about how to make people like you by talking about them," said Mary Anne. "It's great because you always have something to say. You ask the other person questions. You comment on stuff about them. Even personal stuff. The article says people love that. They end up thinking *you're* interesting because you're interested in them. Read it."

"Do you do that with Logan?" I asked.

"No," admitted Mary Anne, stretching out on my bed.

"Then why should I?" I asked, tossing the magazine across the room onto the desk.

"Because Logan likes me the way I am," she said, as she picked up my brush and ran it through her hair. "But you're just getting to know Lewis. After a while you can drop the act."

"Then isn't it sort of false?" I asked.

"Dawn!" cried Mary Anne. "I'm just trying to help you. Do you want Lewis to like you or don't you?"

Before I could answer, Mum called up the stairs. "Mary Anne, phone! It's Logan."

Mary Anne practically flew out of the room. Sitting on the edge of my bed, I began ripping the plaits out of my hair. I didn't want to think about anything. I was in the worst mood ever.

In a few minutes, Mary Anne returned. "Don't worry about a thing," she told me excitedly. "Everything is fine. Logan wants to plan a double date for tomorrow night. I said you'd love to go."

"Does Lewis want to go?" I asked.

"He didn't say no," Mary Anne answered, as she picked up the magazine from the desk. "Here," she said, handing it back to me. "Start reading."

With a sigh, I looked at the article on "you-directed conversation." I read the subtitle. "'Ten great conversation

89

builders.'" I went on. "'One. Everyone loves a compliment . . .'" Settling back on my bed, I continued to read. I had to learn so much by the next night.

9th CHAPTER

Saturday

Food! I sometimes wish it didn't exist. It would be great if we could just take little capsules to keep us alive. And we didn't have any taste buds. And there was no such thing as ice cream or chocolate cake to tempt us. (But since we didn't have taste buds, we wouldn't care, anyway.)

I know I'm supposed to be writing about my babysitting experience, not about food. But my babysitting experience was about food. I sat for Norman Hill.

Apparently the Hills have decided to get tough with Norman. When I arrived at their house,

they had worked out this plan
for him. They told me about it
the minute I walked in the door....

When Stacey reached their house, Mr and Mrs Hill practically pounced on her. They thought Claudia and I had let Norman snack too much. But that wasn't all. They had decided that they, themselves, had been too easy on Norman. He was going to lose weight no matter what it took.

"Here's his new exercise tape," said Mrs Hill, handing a video to Stacey.

"We can do this together," Stacey said to Norman, who was standing beside her in the hall. Norman just looked at her and made a disgusted face.

"His meal plan is pinned to the notice board in the kitchen," added Mr Hill. Both Mr and Mrs Hill were stylishly dressed in expensive-looking sports outfits. Mr Hill wore a black tracksuit. Mrs Hill wore a soft peach outfit. "We'll be at the Fitness Faze health club," said Mr Hill.

"Do *not* let Norman snack on cakes or cookies," Mrs Hill told Stacey. "There are carrot and celery sticks in the fridge if he's hungry." Mrs Hill planted a quick kiss on top of Norman's wispy hair. "Remember, Normie. Lots of water. We want to keep that system flushed."

Dawn

Full name
Dawn Read Schafer

Age
13 years old

Birthday
5th February

Birthplace
California

Club Position
Alternate Officer

Siblings
Ten year old brother Jeff

Best friend
Stepsister Mary Anne

Likes
Health food, sunshine, the
outdoors, ghost stories, and the
movie *The Parent Trap*

Dislikes
Cold weather, junk food, red
meat, and disorganization

First major crush
Travis

Claim to fame
"When I was two, Mum entered
my picture in a baby contest in
Los Angeles and I won."

Dawn in 25 words or less
"I like to think I'm an
individual."

"I'm not a toilet bowl," Norman muttered.

"Oh, Norman." Mrs Hill sighed. "You know what the doctor said. Water fills you up and cleanses impurities from your system."

Mr Hill called to his wife from the bottom of the stairs. "Come on, Michelle."

Mrs Hill turned and hurried to join her husband.

"It won't be so bad," said Stacey, when they'd left. "You know, *I* can't eat sweets. You get used to it after a while."

"Why can't you?" Norman asked. "You're not fat."

Stacey told him about her diabetes. "I don't even have a choice," she said. "I can get really ill if I don't stick to my diet."

"Gee," said Norman sympathetically. "I'd go insane if I were you."

Stacey smiled. "No, you wouldn't. You would do what you had to do. I'm not happy about it. But it's what I have to do."

At that moment, Sarah ran in from her bedroom. "I need food to bring to Elizabeth's picnic."

"Picnic?" asked Stacey. "It's freezing out."

"Elizabeth is having it in her conservatory. It's heated," said Sarah.

"Can I come?" asked Norman.

Sarah's dark eyes shifted back and forth guiltily. "You're not invited. Besides, you have to stick to your diet. Mum and Dad said so."

Norman looked up at Stacey pleadingly. "Can't I go?"

Stacey was on the horns of a dilemma. (I read that phrase once in a book and I try to use it whenever possible. I think it's funny.) Anyway, she didn't want to hurt Norman's feelings, but she thought the Hills *would* be angry if she let him go to a picnic. "Why don't you stay here with me," Stacey suggested. "I want to see that exercise tape. And I don't want to do it alone."

"You *want* to exercise?" Norman questioned.

"Why not?" said Stacey, trying to sound perky. "It's fun. But it's more fun if you do it with someone else. Let's put on the tape right now."

"Okay, I suppose so," agreed Norman, not sounding too enthusiastic.

Stacey went to the living room and stuck the tape in the VCR.

"I'm taking this bunch of bananas," Sarah yelled from the kitchen.

"What's Elizabeth's phone number?" Stacey called back to her.

"It's on the notice board," said Sarah, entering the living room, wearing her coat, the bananas in one hand. "Her name is Elizabeth Yates."

"Don't leave there without phoning me first," Stacey warned.

94

"I won't," said Sarah.

The opening music of the exercise tape had come on. It was lively and fast-paced. Stacey slipped out of her loafers and began hopping around to the music. Sarah stood and watched for a minute. "Come on, Norman," said Stacey. "We're going to have a good time."

From the look on Sarah's face, Stacey could see she was convincing Sarah, but not Norman, that exercising could be fun. "Do you want to stay and exercise with us?" she asked Sarah.

"No," Sarah decided, after considering for a moment.

Norman grabbed the opportunity to give his sister a dig. He smiled and began hopping to the music. "Hey, this *is* fun!" he cried.

With one last look over her shoulder, Sarah left. The minute the door slammed, Norman stopped hopping. And his smile faded. "I need a drink of water," he told Stacey.

Stacey stopped the tape. "All right. Go ahead."

"You don't have to wait for me," Norman told her. "I'll be right back. You can keep exercising."

"No problem," Stacey countered. "I don't mind waiting."

Norman went into the kitchen. Stacey waited. The tap was turned on—but it wasn't turned off. As she listened to the running water, Stacey wondered: Just how much is this kid drinking? She remembered hearing that you're supposed to sip water while exercising, not guzzle it. Norman could develop a cramp.

"Norman," said Stacey, walking towards the kitchen. "Don't drink too much—" She stopped short when she got into the kitchen. The water was running, all right. But Norman wasn't drinking it. He was sitting at the table with a glass of soda in front of him, shovelling crisps into his mouth.

Stacey turned off the tap. Norman gulped down the last of his crisps. "I was a bit hungry," he said meekly.

"And you thought running water would cover the sound of the crunching," Stacey said bluntly.

Norman smiled guiltily. "I couldn't help it. I had to eat."

"Why did you have to?" Stacey challenged him. "Did you have breakfast this morning?"

Norman looked down and nodded.

"Then why can't you wait until lunch?" Stacey pressed.

Suddenly Norman looked up at her. His face was red. "Because I don't feel very happy at the moment. When I get sad I like to eat. Okay?"

"Do you feel sad because of the picnic?" Stacey asked gently.

"I just feel sad," Norman pouted. "I don't know. Maybe it's because of the picnic."

Stacey leaned back against the worktop. "You know, there are other things you can do when you feel sad."

"How would you know?" Norman said, sulking.

"Because sometimes I feel sad, too. Everyone feels sad once in a while."

"Not as much as I do," Norman insisted.

"Okay, apart from kids teasing you and Sarah annoying you, what makes you feel so sad?" Stacey asked. (She already knew about Sarah and the kids from reading the BSC notebook. It *does* come in handy.)

Norman thought a moment. "My mother and father. They don't like me."

Stacey felt her heart twist when Norman said that. How awful for a kid to feel that way. "Of course they like you, Norman," said Stacey. "They love you."

"No, they don't," Norman said, looking at his hands on the table. "They wish I'd never been born."

"Norman, I'm sure that's not true!" cried Stacey.

"It is. They're never at home. That's because they don't want to see me. Once I heard my father say, 'Norman is so fat, I can't believe he's our son.' He doesn't want me to be his son." Norman jammed the palms of his hands into his eyes and brushed away the tears.

"Honestly, Norman, I don't think he meant anything by that," said Stacey. "You should talk to him and tell him how you feel."

"I can't," Norman whined. "He'll think I'm a cissy."

"But if you talk to him he might tell you he loves you and he's proud of you," said Stacey.

"I don't think so," Norman disagreed. "I brought home four E's on my report card this term and he didn't even care. Four excellents!"

"Oh, come on, Norman, I bet he was *very* proud. What did he say?" Stacey asked.

"How come a bright kid like you can't lose some weight?" Norman told her.

Ow! thought Stacey. "What did your mum say?" she asked, hoping for a better response from Mrs Hill.

"She said, 'That's great, Normie! Now all you have to do is get an E for eating excellence.' They only care about my weight."

Stacey felt terrible for Norman. His parents *were* part of his problem—and they didn't even know it.

"I think you should tell your parents how you feel," Stacey suggested. "Tell your mother if you can't tell your father."

"She'll just tell me to flush my system," said Norman glumly.

Stacey was desperate to cheer up Norman. "Here's what you do if she says that," said Stacey. She put her hand to her forehead as if she were saluting. Then she brought her palm and thumb down over her eye as she said, "*Flussshhhhh!*" as if she were a toilet flushing.

Naturally, this cracked Norman up. (When dealing with seven-year-old boys, toilet jokes work almost every time.) He imitated Stacey. "*Flushshhhhh!*" His face beamed with laughter.

Stacey felt slightly guilty about telling Norman to do this. His mother might not appreciate it. Still, she didn't really care. She liked seeing Norman laugh.

10th CHAPTER

By six o'clock on Saturday evening my brain felt as if it were about to explode. I had been given more dating advice than I could handle.

This was thanks to Mary Anne. No sooner had I finished one magazine article than she handed me another. No matter how fast I read, she was always one article ahead of me.

After learning about "you-directed conversations", I read articles with titles like "Taking Charge of Your First Date"; "Flirting With Flair"; "Subtle Signs to Show You Care." One was even called (believe it or not) "Eating Tips for New Daters." (Don't eat things that can get stuck in your teeth or that will give you wind. Wind! I couldn't believe it! Though I suppose belching—or worse—would be totally mortifying.)

I was slowly getting more and more annoyed with Mary Anne. It was hard to confront her, because she *was* trying to help me. But I felt like screaming, "Mary Anne, is *anything* about me okay the way it is?"

There really was no point in asking, though. The answer was obviously no.

I kept telling myself to be grateful for Mary Anne's help. After all, she had a steady boyfriend. She had to know more about it than I did. Still, she was definitely getting on my nerves.

Mary Anne sat on my bed while I got ready for our double date. "Dawn, you're not wearing that, are you?" she asked, as I pulled one of my new tight, lycra skirts out of the wardrobe.

"You said it was nice," I reminded her.

"I know, but not for tonight. You need something special." She was already dressed in a nice flowered dress. Earlier I'd done her hair in a French plait. (It was a little too short for a plait, but with hairgrips, gel, and a bow at the bottom, I made it look nice.) She wore a little blusher, some mascara, and lip gloss. Mary Anne looked pretty, but not especially special.

"Look at you," I pointed out. "You're casual."

"Logan already likes me the way I am," she replied. (I noticed this was the second time she'd said that.) "You're just starting to date Lewis."

I threw up my hands in frustration. "I don't have any other skirts or dresses," I cried. "I mean, I don't have anything special."

"Let me see what I have," said Mary Anne.

As she walked out of the door, I shook my head in disbelief. A year ago I would never (ever) have expected to be taking fashion advice from Mary Anne. Imagine—Mary Anne, the girl who used to wear pinafore dresses and pigtails, was now telling *me* how to dress! It was strange but true.

"Try these," said Mary Anne, returning to the room. She threw a denim skirt and a black poloneck on my bed. I tried them on. I thought I looked kind of plain, but Mary Anne was ecstatic. "Perfect," she proclaimed. "I'm going to phone Logan and tell him we're ready."

I needed more time. But Mary Anne was out of the door before I could say anything.

Standing in front of my mirror, I sighed at my image. Mary Anne was wrong. I *was* too plain. Working quickly, I applied blusher, mascara, and lots of navy blue eyeliner. The final touch was the hot pink lipstick I'd bought at the chemist that afternoon.

The next problem was my hair. Mary Anne had advised me to pull it back, letting curly wisps fall out of the clip. "It's very romantic this way," she said, as she decided which wisps belonged where.

But just that afternoon I'd read a magazine article saying pulled-back hair turned boys off. ("Let him see your feminine glory loose and flowing free," is what it said, to be exact.) So I opened the clip and let the curls "flow free." I looked like a little kid with big loopy curls. Luckily I had some hair gel. I put gel on the sides, and looked a lot better.

I jazzed up the outfit with a pair of black textured stockings I'd bought at Zingy's and a pair of short black boots I already owned. My skirt needed to be shorter, so I rolled it up a bit and untucked the black poloneck. Much better, I decided, as I left my room.

When I met Mary Anne on the stairs, she frowned. "What happened to your hair?"

"I like it better this way," I insisted.

"It's okay, I suppose," she said sceptically. "But you went overboard with the eyeliner."

"If it looks so bad I'll take it off," I snapped, turning on the narrow stairs.

Mary Anne grabbed my arm. "You don't have time. Lewis and Logan are already on their way over. The eyeliner isn't that awful."

"Thanks," I said dryly.

"No, it's fine. You'll just make a big mess if you start to redo it now. We don't want to be late for the film."

"I thought we were eating first," I said.

"Logan and I decided we should eat later," said Mary Anne. "Since we're going earlier, we can catch an earlier film."

"Thanks for telling me," I grumbled.

Mum and Richard were watching TV in the living room. When I came in, Richard frowned. Mum shot him a glance that said, "Leave her alone." I have to give Richard credit (and thank Mum). He didn't say a word. He just pretended to be concentrating on the TV programme.

"Have a good time," Mum said, as the doorbell rang.

"Home by ten,' said Richard, glancing up from the screen.

"You said ten-thirty," Mary Anne reminded him.

"Ten-thirty on the dot," Richard agreed.

Logan stood at the front door, looking pretty much as he always does. ("Exactly like Cam Geary," Mary Anne likes to say.) It probably took him all of ten minutes to comb his hair and put on a clean shirt. Boys have it so easy.

"I like your hair that way," Logan told Mary Anne.

"Thanks," Mary Anne replied, taking his hand. In the drive, Mr Bruno was waiting for us with the motor running. Logan jumped into the front seat, leaving Mary Anne and me in the back with Lewis.

The minute I saw Lewis, that melty,

mushy feeling hit me all over again. He was not only handsome, but he had a pleasant face. He'd seemed nice in his letters, and from his face you could tell he *was* nice. His letters had shown the real Lewis.

"Hi," I said to my date. Then I remembered one of my ten conversation boosters. *Always use the person's name*. "Hi, Lewis," I added quickly.

"He heard you the first time, Dawn," Mary Anne said, with a nervous giggle.

"I know that, Mary Anne," I replied, an edge to my voice.

"Hi!" Lewis laughed. "Are you ready to show me Stoneybrook nightlife?"

"That should take about three seconds." I chuckled. Suddenly I remembered another conversation booster. *Avoid negativity. Be upbeat*. "Actually, there is a great deal to see and do here in Stoneybrook. The nightlife is one of the great things about our town. I'm out practically every night of the week!"

I was stopped cold by the expression on Mary Anne's face. She was looking at me as if I had lost my mind.

"Well, not every night of the week." I giggled. "Many nights, but not every night. I mean—"

"Dawn is joking," Mary Anne interrupted me. "She's always kidding around. Aren't you, Dawn?"

Lewis and Mary Anne both looked at me.

"Yes, I suppose I am," I replied, feeling like a moron. "That's me. A real kidder."

"Dawn, tell Lewis about California," coached Mary Anne.

"California is great," I began. California is a subject I like talking about. "The last time I visited my father and Jeff, I felt as if I'd never left, in some ways. But in other ways I felt a little odd to be back. I think that was because—" I stopped myself. This was all wrong. I wasn't supposed to talk about me. I was supposed to be "you-directed" and talk about Lewis. "I'd much rather hear about Kentucky," I said.

"Logan's probably told you most of it," Lewis said.

Everyone loves a compliment, I recalled. "Tell us about Louisville," I said. "Anywhere *you* live must be totally *fascinating*, Lewis."

I was proud of myself. I'd been "you-directed" *and* delivered a compliment. Plus, I'd thrown Lewis's name in for good measure.

Lewis gave me a wary look. Maybe he wasn't used to such dazzling conversation. "It's not all that fascinating," he began, but he told us about Louisville. I wasn't really listening because I was thinking ahead to the next thing I should say.

Notice something special about the person you're talking to. What could I notice about Lewis? Suddenly I came up with a good

106

one. "Hey, I've just realized something," I blurted out.

"Dawn!" said Mary Anne. (It came out "Daw-aaa-unnnnn!") "Lewis was talking."

"Oh, I'm sorry," I apologized. "It's just that I realized your name is Lewis, and you live in Louisville."

"So?" asked Mary Anne.

"So, Lewis, Louis. Don't you get it?"

Lewis moaned. "Ever since I was little, people have always said: 'Hey, Lewis, do you own the whole town?' Or if I ask a question, they say: 'This is your town, you should know.' It drives me crazy."

"Oops, sorry," I said.

"No, it's okay." Lewis smiled. "You didn't know."

He was *so* nice!

When we reached the cinema, I was surprised to see that *Gone With the Wind* was showing. I'd thought we were going to see a new film that had just come out. One I was really looking forward to. "We're seeing this in honour of Lewis, since he's from the South," Mary Anne said, as we stood in the ticket line.

While the boys bought the tickets, Mary Anne pulled me aside. "This is a very romantic film. That's really why I chose it," she whispered. "When a kissing scene comes, rest your hand near Lewis's. Give him the chance to hold it. Oh, and there are some scary parts in this film. Lean in towards him at those times, as if you're really scared."

"All right," I agreed since Mary Anne seemed to know what she was talking about.

"Anyone want popcorn?" Logan asked, as we passed the snack counter.

"Okay," said Mary Anne.

"How about you?" Lewis asked me.

"No thanks, Lewis," I said, remembering to use his name *and* not to eat anything that might get stuck in my teeth.

Suddenly I felt a sharp pinch on my arm. It was Mary Anne. "Dawn would love some popcorn," she told Lewis. "She adores popcorn. Don't you, Dawn?"

"Oh, yeah. I forgot. I do," I said. (I certainly wasn't impressing Lewis with my brains this evening. But maybe that was okay. Boys aren't supposed to like intelligent girls. That's what I've heard, anyway.)

"I'll get the popcorn, since you paid for the film," I offered. "Ouch!" Mary Anne had pinched me again.

"Are you okay?" Lewis asked me.

"Yes, um, I just had cramp," I lied.

"Oh," Lewis said. "Do you want to go home?" (Oh great! I said to myself. He thinks I'm an invalid.)

"In my leg, that's all," I said, hopping a little for effect.

"She always gets leg cramps," Mary Anne jumped in. "By the time you come back with the popcorn, she'll be fine."

"Okay," said Lewis. He looked worried as he joined Logan at the snack counter.

"Stop pinching me," I hissed at Mary Anne.

"Sorry, but I had to talk to you alone. You have to have popcorn," Mary Anne said impatiently. "That way you can reach for it the same time he does. It's a way for your hands to meet."

When we found our seats, Mary Anne made a big drama out of climbing over Logan so that Lewis and I would be sitting together. Thank goodness the lights finally went down and the film started.

Lewis's idea of sharing popcorn was to hand me the bucket, then take it back. There was no chance of meeting in the middle.

So it was up to me.

When I had the popcorn, I propped it up between us on the arms of the seat and waited. My eyes darted back and forth from the screen to the popcorn. I'd have to be quick if I wanted to get my hand in there at the same time Lewis did.

At last he reached for the popcorn. I went for it at the same time.

But I missed. (Boy, did I miss!)

Instead of gently brushing his hand, I knocked over the bucket. Buttery popcorn flew everywhere. "I'm so sorry," I cried, jumping out of my seat.

"Sit down!" the woman behind me scolded angrily.

On my knees, I began scooping up popcorn.

"Sit down and forget about it," Mary Anne snapped at me.

"Okay," I mumbled, sitting on some popcorn that had landed on my seat.

In the scene where all of Atlanta was burning, I leaned towards Lewis as Mary Anne had instructed. But Lewis was on the edge of his seat, straining forward. He didn't even notice.

And then, as if things weren't bad enough, I started crying when Scarlett and Rhett's little girl fell off the horse and died. Lewis turned and looked at me then. For a moment I thought he was admiring my sensitivity. Wrong.

I discovered what he was really gazing at when I wiped my eyes. Looking down at my hand, I saw that it was navy blue. (Practically.) It was smeared with eye make-up.

"Oh no!" I cried. I jumped up again. Eye make-up was all over my face.

"Sit *down!*" hissed the woman behind me.

"Sorry," I muttered, as I stumbled over a zillion feet on my way to the aisle. In the ladies' room I saw that the mess was even worse than I'd imagined. Blue-black streaked my cheeks. It took forever to mop up. And I had to go through the same thing

110

all over again when Miss Melanie died. (Why couldn't Mary Anne have picked a comedy?)

Gone With the Wind is a long film. By the time we got out, it was nearly ten. "Let's eat something quick at the coffee shop," Logan suggested. "I can phone my father from there."

"I think we'd better go straight home," I said, feeling pretty worn out. "Richard will be cross if we're late."

Reluctantly, Mary Anne agreed. On the journey home, she seemed determined to make the most of the last minutes of our date. "Dawn is so funny sometimes," she told Lewis. "Dawn, tell Lewis what you did on New Year's Eve."

"I don't know what you're talking about," I said.

"Of course you do," replied Mary Anne. "Dawn put up a banner she'd found that said, 'Happy New Year 1979.'"

"I don't get it," Lewis said, bewildered.

"There's nothing to get," said Mary Anne. "It's just that another person wouldn't have put the sign up. But Dawn always does things her own way. She's a real individual."

Lewis gave me that small quavery smile he'd used at the airport. The date was a complete disaster. And Mary Anne was only making it worse.

I thought the journey would never end.

But at last it did. We said goodnight, and Mr Bruno drove off.

"Well," said Mary Anne, as we stood in the drive, waving. "The least you can do is thank me."

"What are you talking about?" I asked.

"I tried as hard as I could to make this date a success. It's not my fault that you did everything wrong. I did the best I could."

"You're right, Mary Anne," I said furiously. "I would like to thank you. Thanks a lot for absolutely nothing!" Tears of anger sprang to my eyes as I turned and stormed into the house.

11th
CHAPTER

On Monday afternoon we held our usual BSC meeting. I had no intention of walking to Claudia's with Mary Anne. If I did, I might have to talk to her. And I had decided never to talk to Mary Anne, the know-it-all Date Wrecker, again.

Mary Anne felt the same way. (Though why *she* should be angry with *me*, I had no idea.) But clearly she no more wanted to talk to me than I wanted to talk to her. Which was just fine.

Even though I gave Mary Anne almost a five-minute head start, I arrived at Claudia's right behind her. (I suppose I do have longer legs than she does.) Mary Anne was only halfway up the stairs when I let myself in the Kishis' front door. Without even looking at Mary Anne, I walked up the stairs and right past her.

"How was the date?" Stacey asked, the

minute I entered Claudia's room. (We had not discussed it at school. The school canteen is not exactly an appropriate place for private conversations.)

"Was it great?" asked Kristy eagerly.

"Tell us about it," Claudia said excitedly.

"There's nothing to tell," I replied, as I sat on Claudia's bed. "Mary Anne interrupted me when I spoke. In front of everyone, she treated me like an idiot. She told stupid stories about me. And she completely ruined my chances with Lewis. That's all."

Mary Anne had come into the room right behind me. Her eyes narrowed and her face turned pink with anger. "Would you like to hear the real story now?" she asked. "The real story is that Dawn made an idiot of herself. I did my my best to stop her. Which is why I *had* to interrupt her sometimes. I told interesting stories about her, since *she* wasn't saying anything interesting."

I pushed up the sleeves of the black leotard I was wearing. "Mal, do you see this black-and-blue mark?"

Mallory winced. "What happened?"

"This is where Mary Anne pinched me every time she didn't like something I said," I pointed out.

"Ouch," said Jessi sympathetically.

"Since Dawn was in her own little world, it was the only way I could get her attention," Mary Anne said, defending herself. "I did all I could to help her, but it was no use. I did her hair, she wrecked it. I picked out a great outfit for her, and she turned it into one of these bizarre new get-ups she's been wearing lately."

Everyone looked at me. I'd spent Sunday tie-dying a pair of white tights and some of Richard's old T-shirts. Today I was wearing the dyed tights, my new lycra skirt, and one of the T-shirts belted over a leotard.

I'd spent the rest of the afternoon putting my hair in tiny plaits all over my head. Then I gelled the plaits. This morning I'd unplaited my hair up to about chin-length. I left in the plaits along my head. It looked cool. The top was in plaits and the bottom was all crinkled and frizzy.

"Ask Dawn what happened to her eye make-up during the film," added Mary Anne.

"What happened to your eye make-up?" Kristy asked me.

"Mary Anne deliberately picked the saddest film of all time so that my make-up would run," I said flatly.

"Ask Dawn who advised her not to wear so much eye make-up," Mary Anne countered.

"Ask Mary Anne who moved the time of the date forward so that I didn't have time to take the eye make-up off," I shot back.

"Ask later," said Kristy. "We have club business to discuss right now."

Mary Anne shot me a nasty look and then opened the record book on her lap. "I'm ready," she said huffily.

"I'd like to talk about the Hills," said Stacey. "Should one of us speak to Mr or Mrs Hill about Norman? They're making him feel terrible, and they don't even know it."

"They might take it the wrong way," suggested Jessi cautiously.

"I agree," Claudia said. "We would be butting into their personal life."

"But we can't just sit back and do nothing," objected Stacey.

"Stacey's right," I spoke up. "Mr and Mrs Hill are making Norman feel worthless. Somebody should say something."

"Who?" Kristy asked.

That was the big question. Nobody volunteered. I certainly didn't want the job. The Hills weren't the kind of people who put you at ease.

"Anybody?" Kristy asked. "I don't know them. Besides, I'm not sure we should interfere."

"It's my idea, so I should be the one," Stacey conceded. "But I'm too chicken. As it is, the Hills make me feel as if I'm bothering them whenever I ask them anything."

"I know what you mean," agreed Claudia. "It's as if they're always too busy or something."

116

"I think Norman feels the same way," I added.

"Let's think about it more before we do anything," said Kristy. "Maybe somebody will come up with a creative solution."

"I hope so," said Stacey.

Just then, Mr Hill phoned. He needed a sitter for Tuesday afternoon. "I'm the only one free," Mary Anne told Kristy, consulting the book. "So I'll check out the situation at the Hills'. Maybe I'll come up with an idea."

"Huh," I snorted doubtfully.

Mary Anne glared at me.

We received two more phone calls. The first was from Mr Prezzioso. Kristy took that job. The second was from Mrs Barrett. "Would someone please tell Dawn that the jobs is hers if she wants it," Mary Anne said stiffly.

For a moment there was silence. Then Kristy sighed loudly. "Dawn, would you like to sit for the Barretts?" she asked.

"Fine with me," I answered.

Mary Anne stared into space as though she hadn't heard me. Kristy sighed again, even louder this time. "Fine with her," Kristy told Mary Anne.

"Thank you." Mary Anne wrote my name in the record book.

The rest of the afternoon didn't go any better. Once we got home, Mary Anne and I would have simply gone on avoiding each other—but our friends had other plans for us.

The first phone call came from Kristy, just before six-thirty. Both Mary Anne and I were in the kitchen, helping with supper. Mum answered the phone and handed it to Mary Anne.

"Uh-huh . . . Okay . . . Uh-huh," Mary Anne spoke into the phone. Then she frowned. "Why do we have to do that?" she asked, sounding annoyed.

I pretended not to pay attention, as I laid the table. But, truthfully, I was dying to know what Kristy was saying. Normally Mary Anne would have stopped her phone conversation to tell me. I wondered if I'd ever find out what they were talking about.

"You can tell her yourself," Mary Anne said to Kristy. After a few minutes she said, "Oh, all right." Putting aside the phone, Mary Anne turned to me. "Get on the extension. Kristy wants to talk to both of us at once."

I picked up the phone in the living room. "Hi, Kristy. What's up?"

"I can't stop thinking about the Hills," she said. "Mary Anne is going over there next, and I was wondering—since you've already been there—if you had any suggestions for her. I haven't sat for the Hills, so I really don't know."

Do you want to know why Kristy is the chairman of our club? This is why. She knows how to get things accomplished. I was now in a spot. If I refused to talk to Mary Anne it meant I was refusing to help Norman. Plus, asking Mary Anne and me to talk over the phone (even though we were just one room apart) was brilliant. It's always easier to talk on the phone.

"I'm not sure," I said slowly. "Maybe Norman has a teacher he likes. You could suggest that he talk to the teacher, and maybe the teacher could talk to the Hills."

"Would we have to get in touch with the teacher?" asked Kristy.

"Maybe," I replied.

"The Hills might get angry if we go to the school behind their backs," Mary Anne pointed out.

"Well then, what if we just encourage Norman to talk to the teacher himself?" Kristy said.

"Do you think he'd do it?" Mary Anne asked.

"I don't know," I replied. There. I'd spoken to Mary Anne. Kristy certainly is clever.

"Why don't you two discuss it some more," said Kristy. (Okay, so she's not too subtle sometimes.) "I'm going to phone Stacey and see what she thinks."

When Kristy had hung up, Mary Anne and I didn't talk. We went back to silently laying the table. In less than five minutes, the phone rang again.

This time I picked up. It was Stacey. "Hi," she said. "I had this idea about the Hills I wanted to talk about."

"What is it?" I asked.

"Put Mary Anne on the extension. Since she's going there next, she should hear this."

I couldn't do that without talking to Mary Anne. "Pick up the extension," I said, staring at the ceiling as I spoke.

In a moment, Mary Anne joined the conversation. "Hi, Stacey."

"Hi. Here's my idea. When I was at the Hills' the last time, I noticed that Sarah was interested in the exercise tape. And Mr and Mrs Hill were on their way out to a health club. I was thinking that if we could get them all to exercise *with* Norman, it would be more fun for him. They'd also spend some time as a family. They could use more of that. I think part of Norman's problem is that he's lonely."

"That's a great idea!" I said sincerely.

"But who's going to tell this to the Hills?" asked Mary Anne. "They don't even know me. I can't just walk in there and start making helpful suggestions."

"Claudia got along well with Sarah. Maybe she can think of something," I said.

Drat! I realized I'd just spoken to Mary Anne again.

Stacey hung up, and in few minutes Claudia called. Once again Mary Anne and

I both got on the phone. Claudia suggested that Mary Anne encourage Sarah and Norman to do something together. "It would be the first step. And keep their neighbour Elizabeth out of the picture if you can."

"Don't be too pushy about it, though," I said. "Everybody in the Hill family is always giving Norman advice. Maybe if they just left him alone he could go about losing weight in his own way. If we're too pushy, we could end up being as bad as Mr and Mrs Hill."

"That's a good point," agreed Mary Anne.

Ha! That time she'd slipped and spoken to me.

Later that night, Mal phoned and suggested working on making a picture book with Norman about an overweight kid who had super powers. "That might boost his self-image," she said.

Jessi called, suggesting that Norman might like dancing better than exercising. "It's just as good for you, and more fun." She had a dancercise tape she said Mary Anne could bring to the Hills' with her.

You have to admit, when the BSC tackles a problem, we do come up with a lot of good ideas.

Speaking of good ideas—I had one just as I was falling asleep that night. In my mind, I was going over all the things that had been said that evening. I remembered saying that maybe everyone should leave Norman alone.

Then I thought of Lewis.

If Mary Anne had left me alone, I could have conducted my date with him my way. I was pretty sure it would have worked out a lot better.

Isn't it funny how you can see things about someone else that you can't see about yourself? I knew Norman needed everyone to stop interfering. But I hadn't realized it was exactly what I needed, too.

I made up my mind. I had to find some way to see Lewis again. Alone.

12th CHAPTER

Tuesday

The Norman situation is out of control. His parents have become diet maniacs. When I reached the Hills', it was worse than anyone had described.

The minute I walked in, Mr Hill began lecturing me and Norman about what Norman could eat and what he couldn't eat. They've put a list of Norman-No foods and Norman-Yes foods on the fridge. He even wanted me to time Norman as he ran up and down the driveway!

I tried to remember

all your ideas for helping out Norman. I couldn't believe how great they sounded when you explained them. And I couldn't believe how hard they were to carry out.

Mary Anne started by trying to interest both Sarah and Norman in Jessi's dancercise tape. "That's not the right tape," Sarah objected. "My father says Norman has to exercise to *his* tape. It's a special tape for fat boys."

Mary Anne ignored Sarah's comment. "Come on, Norman," she said, as the dancercise tape came on. "We can try it this once. It'll be fun."

Norman folded his arms. "I don't dance," he insisted.

"I'm a bit shy about dancing, too," Mary Anne admitted. "But no one is around to see us."

"No way," said Norman. "Dancing is for cissies."

"Then *you* should love to dance," said Sarah. "Because you're the most enormous cissy there is."

"That's not nice," Mary Anne said.

Sarah shrugged. "He is a cissy and he is enormous. It's not my fault." With her nose up in the air, Sarah turned and went to her room.

Next, Mary Anne tried Mal's picture book idea. At first, Norman was excited. But the idea hit a snag because Mary Anne isn't the greatest artist in the world. "Why are you drawing a balloon with a head?" Norman asked suspiciously.

"Ummmm . . . I suppose I was just drawing a cloud," Mary Anne said. She decided to drop the idea before she unintentionally hurt Norman's feelings.

While Mary Anne and Norman sat at the kitchen table, putting away their coloured pens, Sarah came in. She taped onto the fridge a picture she'd drawn. It was a drawing of a pig. Over it were written the words, "I'm Fat Becuz I Eat Two Much."

"Sarah, please take that down," Mary Anne scolded gently.

"I'm trying to help Norman," said Sarah. "Every time he goes to the fridge, he'll see the fat pig and it will stop him from eating."

"I'm not sure that's a good idea," said Mary Anne.

"*I* think it is," Sarah replied. "My mother says our family has to work together to help Norman with his problem."

Sarah left the kitchen, and in a moment she came back and taped up another drawing. This one was of a big hill with two eyes. The words "Enormous Hill" were written on top.

"That's not helping, Sarah," said Mary Anne.

"Yes, it is," Sarah disagreed. "Norman has to learn not to be a glutton. That's what my father says he is. A glutton."

Mary Anne got really angry. "Norman, why do you let her say such horrible things to you?" she asked, when Sarah had left the kitchen.

Norman shrugged. "What can I do about it? I could tell my parents. They might tell her to stop, but she won't."

"Why don't *you* tell her to stop?"

"She wouldn't listen."

"Make her listen," Mary Anne urged him. "Show her how angry you are."

"I'm not allowed to hit her," Norman said.

"You don't have to. But you can stand up to her."

"How?"

"For starters, you can rip up these pictures." Norman's eyes grew wide. "Yeah?"

"Yeah."

Slowly, Norman got up from the table. "Which one should I rip?" he asked.

"Do you think either of them should be on the fridge?" Norman shook his head. "Then get rid of both of them," said Mary Anne.

Norman approached the pictures cautiously. Keeping his eyes on Mary Anne, he

126

ripped in half the picture of the pig. A big smile crossed his face. He ripped it in half again.

Just then, Sarah returned with *another* drawing in her hand. "My picture!" she shrieked.

Norman took the other one off the fridge. Rip! He tore that one in two.

"Norman! I'm telling!" Sarah cried.

Rip! Ripripripriprip! Norman tore the picture into shreds. "And if you draw any more stupid pictures of me, I'm going to rip them, too!" he yelled.

Sarah's jaw dropped.

She looked at Mary Anne. "Did you hear what he said?"

"I think you'd better not draw any more pictures of him," said Mary Anne, trying not to smile.

Sarah folded her arms tightly across her chest. Turning with a flourish, she stormed off and slammed her bedroom door loudly behind her.

Norman was still red-faced and heaving with anger. "How did I do?" he asked Mary Anne.

"You were great! You were greater than great!"

Norman's face beamed with delight. "I think I'll just rip this list of Norman-No Foods off the fridge, too," he said, boldly.

Gently, Mary Anne caught his hand as he

went for the list. "I think you should wait until your parents get home for that."

"But they won't let me do it then," Norman objected.

"How about this? Why don't you tell your parents that you want to rip this stuff down. Tell them that it makes you angry. Could you do that?"

Norman looked at the shredded picture on the floor. "Maybe I could."

"I know you're brave enough," said Mary Anne, stooping to pick up the pieces of the picture. "Look how you stood up to Sarah."

"That's true," Norman agreed, as he helped pick up the pieces and threw them in the dustbin.

"Are you in the mood for that dancercise tape now?" Mary Anne asked. "We don't have to do it exactly the way it's shown. We can just mess around."

"All right," Norman agreed.

Norman and Mary Anne were both feeling pretty good. They jumped up and down to the beat of the tape, not really dancing, but having fun.

After about five minutes, Sarah came out of her room. She stood in the doorway and watched Mary Anne and Norman as they jumped and laughed. Without saying anything, she joined them.

"Hey, look at me!" Norman said. "This

is a helicopter step I invented." Spreading his arms, he spun around the room.

Sarah grabbed one of her ankles and hopped across the room on one foot. "This is the pogostick dance," she said, giggling.

Mary Anne kept hopping as she watched Norman and Sarah invent one silly dance after another. She loved seeing the two kids getting on so well.

Mary Anne told me later that I had been right. Norman needed some space so he could enjoy who he was. With everyone harping on his faults, no one—not even Norman himself—could see his good points.

Suddenly Mary Anne stopped hopping. Another thought had occurred to her. Was that what she'd done to me?

She hadn't meant to. But maybe she had done it, just the same.

13th CHAPTER

I knew Mary Anne would be babysitting for the Hills on Tuesday afternoon, so that was the perfect time to try to see Lewis alone. No way could Mary Anne pop up and ruin things all over again.

The trouble was, I didn't have the nerve to call. But I was working on it.

Hoping that Lewis would agree to see me after school (if I ever phoned), I took a lot of time dressing on Tuesday morning. I wore my lycra skirt, my tye-dyed tights, and one of my off-the-shoulder tops. My make-up was perfect, and I revived my plaits and frizz hairdo with some gel. With my rubber bracelets and feather earrings in place, I was ready to see Lewis again.

Or maybe I wasn't.

It was just so hard to make that call. I didn't expect Lewis to be thrilled to hear from me. Not after Saturday's dating disaster. But I didn't have anything to lose.

Before lunch, I stopped at the pay phone in the school reception area. "Just do it," I muttered to myself, as I dropped the money in the slot and punched in Logan's phone number.

Mrs Bruno answered and she called Lewis to the phone. "Hi, it's Dawn," I said. My voice was actually shaking. It was so embarrassing.

"Hi, Dawn," said Lewis. (I could almost see him giving me that quivery smile over the phone.)

"Look, Lewis, I know that our date on Saturday didn't go very well," I said, speaking quickly. "But I think things might be better if we met alone. Just the two of us."

"Well, umm . . . okay . . . I suppose," Lewis stammered. (He didn't sound as if he thought this was a super idea.) "Okay. Why not?"

This wasn't the enthusiastic reaction I'd hoped for. But it would have to do.

"Meet me at the coffee shop by the cinema," I suggested. "You know, the one we were supposed to go to after the film. Do you think you can find it?"

"I think so," he said. "What time?"

"Three-fifteen."

"All right. See you then."

That hadn't been so hard. (My heart was

only pounding a million beats a second.) At least it was done. And now I'd get a second chance to make Lewis like me.

I joined my friends (and my ex-friend, Mary Anne) at lunch. I was dying to tell them about Lewis, but I couldn't. Because then I'd have to tell Mary Anne. If I did that, I was sure she would find some way to foul things up. She'd probably drop by with Sarah and Norman, or tell Logan to follow us. I wasn't taking any chances.

At three o'clock, I slammed my locker shut and raced out of the door. When I arrived at the coffee shop, Lewis was already sitting in a booth. He looked extremely uncomfortable as he played with the straw in his lemonade.

"Hi, Lewis," I said, remembering to use his name. "You look very handsome today." (I wanted to get the compliment out of the way early.)

"Thank you," he said, giving me the old quivery smile. (I hoped he would say something about how I looked, but he didn't.) "I got some menus," he said, pushing one towards me.

"I'm not hungry," I said. "I'll just have a lemonade." ("Eating Tips" had recommended not ordering much. Boys expected girls to have dainty appetites.)

Lewis looked disappointed. "Then I won't have anything, either."

We looked at one another for a long,

awkward moment. "Well, here we are," I said, just to break the silence.

"Yup. We're here," Lewis agreed.

More silence.

Suddenly the situation seemed too stupid for words. Who was I trying to kid? Only myself. I couldn't keep up this new image. It was too much work. And obviously I wasn't very good at it. I caught sight of myself in a mirrored panel on the wall. The truth was that I didn't really like the way I looked. "Lewis," I said. "I owe you an apology. A big apology."

"You do?"

"Yes. You see, I've been trying to make you think I'm attractive and sophisticated. But I'm not. I'm sorry. I just wanted you to like me."

"Wait a minute," said Lewis. "Could you run that by me that one more time? I'm totally confused."

"I don't blame you," I said. "The thing is, I don't really look like this."

"What do you really look like?" asked Lewis. "Are you an alien life-form and this is just your human cover?"

"No." I laughed. "I really look like the plain girl in the first photo of me you received."

"I liked the way you looked in that photo," said Lewis.

"You did?" I asked, surprised.

"Yeah. A lot. Why did you change?"

"I just wanted to be different."

"Different how?"

"Cool," I replied.

Lewis threw his head back and laughed. "That certainly explains a lot," he said. "I couldn't work out how you could write such sweet letters and then be so . . . I don't know . . ."

"Weird?" I supplied.

"All right, yeah. Weird," Lewis agreed.

"You really thought I was attractive before?" I asked shyly.

Lewis stopped laughing, but his dark eyes were bright and happy. "I thought you were the prettiest girl I'd ever seen. I was counting the minutes until I could meet you."

"Do you think we could start again?" I asked.

"That's a great idea."

"Could you come to my house in an hour?"

"Don't you want me to walk you home?"

"No," I said, getting up. "I don't want you to see me like this one more second. Just come to my house."

"See you in an hour," said Lewis.

I couldn't get home fast enough. I slammed the door behind me and raced up the stairs. The first thing I did was turn on the shower. I stepped out of my clothes and into the shower. I washed off all the make-up and then unbraided the top of my hair.

Then I rinsed out my hair and wrapped it in a towel.

Pulling on my robe, I dashed to my room and dug in the back of my wardrobe. Luckily I still owned a few clothes that I hadn't "revamped." I found a pair of faded blue jeans and a sweat shirt I'd bought in California that said "U.C.L.A." on it. (That stands for University of California in Los Angeles.) Next I blow-dried my hair and let it fall naturally.

"Welcome back," I said to my image in the mirror. I turned to leave, then I turned round again. I applied a little mascara. I put on a touch of lip gloss, too. That was okay. I still looked like me.

Nobody was at home, so I had the kitchen to myself. I took some parsley from the fridge and chopped it in the food processor. I added olive oil, bulgar wheat, lemon juice, and chopped onion, to make tabouhli salad. Then I put the tabouhli in the fridge. After that I made up a platter of whole wheat crackers, chopped carrots, and celery. I set out a bowl of babaganoush (that's baked, mashed aubergine with tahini sauce and spices) and a plate of hummus (that's mashed chick-peas with spices).

Here was my plan. No boys were allowed in when Mum and Richard weren't at home. So I'd go for a walk with Lewis until a quarter to five. Richard had said he was going to be home early that day. Early

135

means about four-thirty. I could invite Lewis in then, and show him how good health food could be.

I had just finished when the doorbell rang. The minute I opened the door and saw Lewis's smile, I knew things were going to be all right. The quivery, quavery smile was gone. He now wore the wonderful, warm smile I'd seen in his photo. "Hi, Dawn. I'm Lewis," he said.

"Nice to meet you, Lewis," I replied, extending my hand. "Do you feel like talking a walk with me? I'll show you the old barn on our property, if you're interested."

"I'm interested," he said.

We walked to the barn. I told him all about the secret passage and how it was probably part of the Underground Railroad. I showed him the trapdoor inside, to which the passage led.

"This reminds me of the place where we used to spend summers," he said, settling back in the hay. "It was a horse farm about two hours outside Louisville." He told me about the wonderful summers he and Logan had shared on the farm. I laughed when Lewis described how years ago, he had tricked Logan into believing he was the ghost of a dead horse.

"We were such crazy little kids," said Lewis with a laugh. "I'd sit under his bedroom window, whinny, and say, 'You will neeeeeiiigggh-ver leave this farm alive.' "

"Poor Logan." I chuckled.

"Poor Logan, nothing. He got me back. One night he came to the window and dumped a bucket of oats on my head."

It was really easy to talk to Lewis. We laughed so much that before I knew it, it was five o'clock and Richard had arrived home. "Hey, remember in my letters I promised to convert you to health food?" I said.

"I remember, but I was hoping you'd forgotten." Lewis cringed.

"Come on," I said, scrambling to my feet. "You're going to love it."

"I'm not sure."

"If you don't like it, I'll make you a hamburger," I said confidently (praying I wasn't wrong).

Well, guess what. I wasn't wrong. Lewis loved the food, especially the babaganoush. "Do you still want a hamburger?" I asked him.

"Nope," he answered, wiping his mouth. "I'm too full."

Just then we heard the front door open and close. Mary Anne was back. You should have seen her face when she walked into the kitchen. She looked totally shocked and confused.

"Dawn has been introducing me to health food," said Lewis happily.

"I see," said Mary Anne. "Did you like it?"

"Yeah. Surprisingly, I did," Lewis admitted. "But I'd better be going."

"I'll walk you to the door," I told Lewis, standing up.

At the door, Lewis took my hand. "This was a great first date. It was better than I'd imagined. Would it be okay if I come round again tomorrow?"

"I have a BSC meeting until six," I said. "But can you come over in the evening?"

"Drat!" said Lewis. "My aunt and uncle are dragging me out to see some relatives. What about Thursday?"

"Thursday is good," I said.

"Great. We'll do something special."

As I stood at the door, watching him walk down the drive, I realized my dream had come true. Lewis liked me. And he liked me just the way I was.

I shut the door and realized something else. Something less pleasant. Sooner or later I was going to have to talk to Mary Anne. I decided it might as well be sooner.

14th CHAPTER

That evening, I was too full to eat dinner. But I sat at the table and picked, since Richard likes us to have meals together whenever possible.

Dinner was quiet. Mum and Richard seemed tired from work. Mary Anne and I were still not talking to each other.

As soon as the dishes were washed and put away, Mary Anne went upstairs. I was right behind her.

"We have to talk," I said, stepping into her bedroom.

To my surprise, she agreed. "Do you want to go first?"

"Okay," I replied. "As you could see today, Lewis likes me the way I am. Or the way I was before I started taking advice from you. You gave me some really crummy advice, Mary Anne!"

"You were the one who wanted a new

image," Mary Anne reminded me. "I didn't start that."

"I know, but you told me it was a great idea. And then you started giving me all those magazines. Not to mention all the stupid dating tips. Why didn't you just leave me alone?"

"I should have," said Mary Anne.

"What?" That wasn't what I expected her to say.

"You're right. I should have left you alone. I was just so sure you and Lewis could be a great couple that I went overboard. I wanted everything to be perfect. Now I see I was stupid."

"What made you realize that?" I asked.

"Believe it or not, it was Norman Hill," Mary Anne told me as she sat on her bed. "If the Hills weren't so obsessed with getting him to lose weight, they might notice all the likable things about Norman. Seeing him made me realize that, in a way, I was doing the same thing with you."

Tears sprang to my eyes. "You know what really hurt me the most?" I said in a choked voice. "I felt as if you didn't think there was anything to like about me. You thought I should look different and act different. If you had just said, 'You're fine the way you are,' maybe I wouldn't have done all those stupid things."

Mary Anne burst into tears. "Oh, Dawn, I like everything about you," she said. "But

I don't know any more about what boys like than you do. I struck it lucky with Logan, that's all. So I was guessing about what Lewis would like, the same as you. I just wanted everything to be perfect."

"You mean you never used the popcorn trick?" I asked.

Mary Anne wiped her eyes. "No. I had read about it in a magazine that afternoon. Since you've never had a boyfriend, I thought maybe you did need some changes to make Lewis like you. What did I know? But you're just fine as you are."

"Lewis thinks so, too," I said.

"I see that. I think we both under-estimated him. We were treating him like 'a boy' instead of like Lewis. I'm sorry, Dawn."

"I'm sorry, too. It's my fault as much as yours. Maybe even more." Mary Anne and I hugged, sniffling. It was good to be friends again.

"I feel bad that we wasted so much of Lewis's visit. He's leaving on Friday night," said Mary Anne.

Friday night! That seemed impossible. I'd waited so long for his visit, and now it would soon be over.

"Logan and I had such great plans, too," said Mary Anne, flopping back onto her bed.

"Maybe we can still have one really good night out," I suggested. "Lewis and I have a

141

date for Thursday night. Do you want to try for another double date?"

Mary Anne's eyes brightened. "Are you sure that's what you want?"

"If you don't try to control it, and you don't talk for me, and don't tell me what to do. Especially if you don't pinch me," I answered sternly.

"Sorry about that," Mary Anne apologized, wincing at the memory. "I promise not to do any of those things. Do you want to go to see another film?"

"No. We'd waste two whole hours not being able to talk," I objected. My time with Lewis was too short to spend sitting in silence. "What about bowling?"

"Isn't that too uncool?" Mary Anne asked sceptically.

That made me laugh. Being cool was the last thing I wanted to think about right now. "It doesn't matter at this point," I said. "Besides, it might be fun."

"You're right. Since you—and now Lewis—are health food nuts, we can go to Cabbages and Kings to eat," said Mary Anne, naming my favourite restaurant.

"Would Logan be willing to do that?" I asked.

"I think so. I'll ask. It's my way of making it up to you a little bit."

"Thanks," I said. "It *is* a nice restaurant. I'm sure you and Logan would find something you like. The soyaburgers are really good."

"We'll manage," said Mary Anne. (She blanched.)

On Wednesday evening, the four of us got on the phone and arranged our date. After a little coaxing, Logan agreed to go to Cabbages and Kings. And everyone liked the bowling idea. We decided to meet straight after school, so we could spend the longest possible amount of time together.

I hadn't bowled for ages. But apparently Lewis and Logan had gone bowling together lots of times in Louisville. Their fathers were even in the same bowling league. The boys were really good.

The big surprise was Mary Anne. She'd only bowled four times before, but she was great. She ended up with the highest score of anyone! (Lewis and I played as a team, and Mary Anne and Logan were another team. As I said, Mary Anne was the best. Then Lewis. Then Logan. Then me. Bowling doesn't seem to be my talent. But I didn't care. It was fun.)

At one point I took Mary Anne aside and whispered, "I read a magazine that says you're not supposed to beat your boyfriend at sports. It damages his ego."

Mary Anne knew I was teasing. "When we go home, let's dig a big hole and dump those magazines into it," she said, smiling.

"We can't. They're Stacey's," I reminded her.

"Then we'll give them back tomorrow."

After bowling we had the nicest time at Cabbages and Kings. Of course, Mary Anne, Logan, and Lewis kidded me whenever possible. "Where's the seaweed?" asked Logan. "I was looking forward to a nice seaweed sandwich."

"Seaweed is out of season," Mary Anne told him seriously. "But you might like the red ants. They're very high in protein and fibre."

Lewis pretended to lift his shirt. "Perhaps we should put some salt on my shirt and eat it. It's loaded with fibre."

"Very funny." I laughed. "The food here is good." I didn't mind the teasing. Everyone was in a terrific mood and we laughed a lot. In the end, Logan and Mary Anne claimed to like the soyaburgers they'd ordered. Lewis raved about his vegetable and pine nut casserole in cheese sauce. (I think I may have converted him to healthy eating.) And my barbecued tofu was terrific.

"Should we phone my father?" Mary Anne asked, when everyone had finished their dessert of red bean ice cream. (Which is really great!)

We looked at one another. Richard would soon be picking us up. Once he arrived, the date would be over.

"We still have a bit of time," said Lewis. "Why don't we go for a walk around town for a while?"

We agreed that that was a good idea. It had got pretty cold outside, and a freezing wind was rushing up the street. But nobody seemed to mind. (Okay, *I* minded. But not enough to want to end the date.) We strolled along, stopping to browse in the windows of the well-lit shops.

While we were looking in the window of an antique shop, Mary Anne suddenly grabbed Logan's sleeve. "Come with me," she said. "I want to show you something in the window of Bellair's." (Bellair's is a big department store, which was just up the street.)

"What is it?" asked Logan.

"I'll show you," Mary Anne insisted, pulling Logan away. Lewis and I started to follow, but Mary Anne shouted, "We'll be right back."

Lewis and I stood in front of the antique shop, our hands jammed into our coat pockets. "I can never get used to this bitter cold," I admitted, shivering. "You're from the South. Is it warmer in Louisville?"

"Only about ten degrees on average," Lewis told me.

"Ten degrees is ten degrees." I laughed. "I wouldn't mind having an extra ten degrees right now."

Lewis wrapped his arms around me. "We

can huddle together for warmth," he said with a smile.

Even though I'm tall, Lewis is taller. I fit neatly under his arm. He was right. I was warmer. But that wasn't really why I felt so good. It was wonderful standing there with Lewis's arms around me.

Then something even more wonderful happened.

Lewis kissed me. And I kissed him back.

I can't describe it to you. (But I'll try.) It was as if time stood still and there was nothing else in the world but Lewis and me. There was only warm breath and two cold noses. Just me and Lewis, holding each other tight.

When the kiss ended, Lewis kept his arms around me. I looked up into his brown eyes. "I'm so glad I got to meet the real Dawn," he said.

"I'm glad, too."

"Your first picture didn't lie," he added. "You *are* the prettiest girl I've ever seen. And you're as nice as your letters."

"So are you," I said. (Not because *Everybody loves a compliment*, but because I meant it.)

Lewis and I might have stood there holding each other forever (or until we turned into ice sculptures), but Mary Anne and Logan returned. "We'd better phone home," said Mary Anne regretfully. "It's starting to get late."

"You're right," I agreed sadly. As we walked to the pay phone on the street, Lewis and I held hands.

It's funny how life works out. I'd planned to make Lewis like me as practice for finding another (local) boyfriend. But as we stood in the cold, waiting for Richard to pick us up, I couldn't imagine ever wanting to kiss anyone *but* Lewis.

15th CHAPTER

HI, DAWN!

WELL, I'M BACK IN LOUISVILLE. AND MISSING YOU ALREADY. I TOOK A BOOK OF VEGETARIAN RECIPES OUT OF THE LIBRARY. MY MUM THOUGHT I'D GONE LOONEY TUNES WHEN SHE SAW ME BAKING SPINACH PIE. SHE ASKED ME: "WHAT DID THEY DO TO YOU UP THERE IN STONEYBROOK?" SO I TOLD HER: "DAWN IS A REALLY INTER-ESTING GIRL. SHE JUST GOT ME THINKING THAT'S ALL."

YOU DID MAKE ME THINK ABOUT A LOT OF THINGS. BUT MOSTLY I THINK ABOUT YOU. I CAN'T WAIT TO SEE YOU AGAIN. BEING SO FAR APART IS HARD, BUT WE'LL MANAGE SOMEHOW. MAYBE WE CAN WORK SOMETHING OUT DURING THE SUMMER.

UNFORTUNATELY, MY MATHS BOOK IS

IN FRONT OF ME, DEMANDING TO BE
OPENED. I'D BETTER GET TO IT. WRITE SOON.
YOURS,
LEWIS

Dear Lewis,
 Hi! I'm sitting for Norman
and Sarah Hill again. (Remember
I told you about them?) For
now, all is quiet. Sarah is at a
neighbour's house (the dreadful
Elizabeth) and Norman is
writing to his pen pal, Brittany.
So things are calm and I
can write.
 I miss you, too. I'm glad I
came to my senses in time
and stopped acting like such
a phoney. When I think about
the things I did, I could die.
You might have gone home
believing I was the strange
person I appeared to be at
first. You never would have
written to me again. What a
horrible thought!
 I agree. We have to find a
way to meet again. Summer is
probably best. Can you come back?

Mary Anne and I have been getting along better than ever since our fight ended. Do you know what she wanted to show Logan in the shop window? Nothing. It was just an excuse to give us time alone. I suppose Mary Anne was interfering again, technically. But this time, I'm glad she did.

I just heard the front door open. Sarah is home. Norman's bedroom door just opened, too. I'd better end this letter. Write real real real real real soon.

       Dawn

P.S. Did you like the spinach pie? Are you brave enough for tofu?

I finished the letter just in time. Sarah came stomping into the living room. She was fuming with anger. "What happened?" I asked.

"Elizabeth is a fish-breathed dweeb!"

True, I thought. "What did she do?"

"She called Norman that name, Enormous Hill, one time too many." As she spoke, Norman appeared behind her. He stopped and listened. "I told her to stop it,"

Sarah continued. "Norman may be fat, but he *is* my brother."

I cast a glance over Sarah's shoulder at Norman. He chewed on his lower lip but didn't say anything. "What did Elizabeth do?" I asked.

"She kept yelling 'Enormous Hill, Enormous Hill' over and over again. So I pushed her. She fell on her bottom into a pile of snow!"

"All right!" Norman cheered. "All right! All right! All right!"

Sarah smiled primly. "She deserved it."

I probably shouldn't have, but I couldn't help smiling. Elizabeth did deserve it. I even wished I had been there to see it. (But then I would have had to scold Sarah, so it was better that I wasn't there.)

Sarah looked down at the wet bottoms of her jeans. "I'm going to change," she said, heading out of the living room.

When I'd arrived at the Hills' that day, I'd noticed a big change. All the diet stuff had been removed from the walls. Now here was another change. Sarah was sticking up for Norman.

Then came the most surprising change of all.

"Would you take my picture?" Norman asked, handing me his parents' Polaroid camera. "Brittany wants a photo of me."

"Of course," I agreed. "Why don't you stand over there by the window?" You

151

should have seen Norman. He was too adorable for words. He posed proudly for the picture, lifting his chin and smiling his sweet smile.

We sat on the sofa and waited for the picture to develop. "So how's it going, Norman?"

Norman checked to see if Sarah was near. She was still in her room. "Great," he said to me in a low voice. "Ever since I ripped up some snotty pictures she drew, Sarah has been much nicer to me. Isn't that weird? I thought she would be meaner than ever. Why is she being so nice?"

"I'm not sure," I admitted. "But maybe since you showed her you have self-respect, she has more respect for you. It works that way sometimes."

"Weird," Norman said. "Guess what else. That night Sarah told my parents what happened. They asked me about it and I told them I got angry when everyone teased me about my weight all the time. I told them it made me want to eat more."

"Did they understand?"

"I think so. They took all that stuff off the walls, and they haven't said a word about me being fat. I know they're still thinking about it, though."

"Really? How do you know that?" I asked.

"Because there are no more treats in the

house. My mother stopped buying biscuits, lemonade, and cake."

The photo was becoming clear. I handed it to Norman and he stared at it for a moment. "I wrote to Brittany about the photo. I told her that even though I'm fat now, I won't be by the summer. I'll send her a new photo then."

"How are you going to lose the weight?" I asked carefully. I didn't want to sound doubtful or discouraging.

"I'm going to pretend I'm Stacey," he told me.

"You're what?"

"I'm going to pretend that if I eat anything sweet, I'll get really ill. Do you think it will work?"

"If you stick with it," I replied. "That's clever of you, Norman."

He nodded. "I know. I'm pretty sure I won't be going to fat camp this summer." Norman looked at the photo again. "Do you think Brittany will stop writing when she sees this?"

"No," I said. "I bet she'll see what I see here."

"What? A fat kid?"

"No," I scoffed, pushing him playfully. "I see a warm smile, intelligent eyes, and a determined attitude. The real Norman shines through in this picture."

Norman smiled at me. "Thanks." He got

up from the sofa. "I have to put this in with my letter."

Just then the phone rang. It was Mary Anne. "Hi," she said, "I just had to call and tell you my news. Logan got a letter from Lewis. He is totally crazy about you. Logan said he went on and on about how great he thinks you are."

"He did?" I asked happily.

"Yeah. He told Logan he's never met a girl who is so honest and interesting. This is a quote from his letter. He said: 'Dawn is the most unique person I've ever met.'"

"Wow!" I cried. "He really did like me the way I am."

"He really did," Mary Anne agreed.

So Norman wasn't the only one who was learning lessons. I'd learned a couple in the last few days, too.

Lewis liked me. As me. I should have more confidence in myself.

I'm glad Lewis got to know the real me because I found out the real me is special. Just like Lewis.

Babysitters MYSTERY

Our favourite Babysitters are detectives too! Don't miss the new series of Babysitters Club Mysteries:

Available now:

No 1: Stacey and the Missing Ring
When Stacey's accused of stealing a valuable ring from a new family she's been sitting for, she's devastated – Stacey is *not* a thief!

No 2: Beware, Dawn!
Just *who* is the mysterious "Mr X" who's been sending threatening notes to Dawn and phoning her while she's babysitting, *alone*?

No 3: Mallory and the Ghost Cat
Mallory thinks she's solved the mystery of the spooky cat cries coming from the Craine's attic. But Mallory can *still* hear crying. Will Mallory find the *real* ghost of a cat this time?

No 4: Kristy and the Missing Child
When little Jake Kuhn goes missing, Kristy can't stop thinking about it. Kristy makes up her mind. She *must* find Jake Kuhn . . . wherever he is!

No 5: Mary Anne and the Secret in the Attic
Mary Anne is curious about her mother, who died when she was just a baby. Whilst rooting around in her creepy old attic Mary Anne comes across a secret she never knew . . .

Look out for:

No 6: The Mystery at Claudia's House
No 7: Dawn and the Disappearing Dogs
No 8: Jessi and the Jewel Thieves
No 9: Kristy and the Haunted Mansion
No 10: Stacey and the Mystery Money